Sinful Vow

Emily Bowie

CONTENTS

Sinful Vow

Luca Rossi isn't my fiancée.

He stole me in the middle of the night.

Now, I'm expected to marry the enemy.

Luca Rossi is the heir to my family's greatest rival within the Italian mafia. He's cocky, ruthless and has a keen sense of when I need him the most.

When I look into his eyes, I see his hatred for what I represent. While I see another arrogant mafia man trying to control me.

On the eve of my arranged marriage, he's the last person I expect to see. Like the thief he is, he steals me in the night, setting off a war that had been brewing for years.

CHAPTER 1

LUCA AGE 10

MY HAND STRETCHES THE yellow-colored elastic that's attached to my homemade wooden slingshot. The sky is hazy with a wildfire thousands of miles away, giving the day an orange glow. There isn't a breath of wind to carry any of the smoke away or to fight against the rock nestled in my pocket.

I eye my surroundings. Two men are dressed in expensive suits, sitting at a cramped table outside near the perimeter of the brick patio. Their bodyguards stand with their hands behind their backs, watching over the street and not toward the bush I'm hiding behind. My hand is bruised and busted from a fight I got into earlier in the week. Each time I pull at the elastic, I'm forced to stare at the injury, causing my mind to be distracted with the way I'm forced to live right now.

My punishment for fighting is no dinner for the next week. They can't beat me—for the most part—because the bruises will show. I'm a lot bigger than I was a year ago. Each year, I become stronger, and soon no one will be able to touch me. At the age of ten, I've now been placed in sixteen different foster homes. It has come to the point when I run away, they don't search for me until a couple of days before the monthly inspection. I'm a scrawny, scrappy, mouthy, dirty kid who no one loves. Not that I need love. I've become good at making the best out of my situation. I can take care of myself.

The two men smell of wealth, and I set my sights on them. Their gold rings and fancy cars showcase their money all the way from over there. I bet they have hundreds in their wallets. My stomach grumbles at the thought of what I could do with that money. Even once it's split three ways.

This street is typically packed with people, which is the reason why I picked it. Busy means it is easier to steal; it's as simple as that. Today, there are small clusters of people around, who seem to belong to these guys and no one else. The sidewalks are empty, and there is a weird vibe in town, similar to when a foster dad gets drunk and is wanting a fight. I don't have time to wait for a better time in the day.

My stomach grumbles, and my legs shake, making my accuracy less than ideal. My concentration is lacking, as all my brain wants to do is scream for food. Glancing back at the two men, I see they're still sitting at the edge of a patio, making it easy to get in and out. The edge of the building shields my two friends, while the green bushes act as a barrier for me.

These two kids who follow me around, I've made them my right-hand men. We all come from broken homes, making us the only family we have. I line my slingshot up, aiming an odd-shaped pebble. My friends are waiting to pickpocket the unsuspecting "too rich for their own good" type of guys as soon as they become startled and stand up. We've done this a hundred times before. It should be like taking candy from a baby.

I have almost perfect aim as I line my shot up. It would be perfect if I had control over the rocks I could find. Some of them have a mind of their own. With their weird shapes and sizes, it can make even the best marksmen inaccurate.

Pulling the elastic back, I keep both eyes open, and the worn leather-like pouch sits next to my cheek as I aim my shot. Deliberately, my fingers let go, and I watch the rock sail through the air. It knocks the hat off the first man, making him draw his gun and stand up.

His eyes are searching, and my friends, Scott and Jay, freeze. None of us were expecting guns. I thought these men were the pushover type who would be frightened. These men don't appear to be panicked. I've never backed down from anyone. Instinctively, I grab another rock and sail it through the air, hitting the man in the back of his head.

The second man stands, moving his coat to show he's packing as well. His demeanor appears to be more amused than angry, unlike the other guy. But I guess it's because I haven't hit him with a rock yet.

Taking another pebble, I move my position and aim for the second guy's hat. They were both wearing brimmed hats, much like the gangsters do in the old movies I've watched. Maybe that should have been a clue that these guys weren't normal businessmen. Pulling the elastic farther back than before, I sail my rock in the air, only for the man to shoot it like a flying clay object. It explodes in the air, impressing me.

His eyes follow the trajectory and land on me before replacing his gun to his side. By now, everyone has scrambled away, because they're all weak. I stand my ground, walking toward them with my head up. They haven't asked me to come, but I go with Plan B, which is to gain their respect. I recognize their type. They have power and money—both things I want to possess. They can't do much more to me than what the world already has.

The man I hit grabs me by the back of the neck and squeezes like you would the scruff of a dog. My arms come out swinging, hoping to hit him hard. I've got practice in fighting bigger men than me. I use my size to my advantage. Curse words are flying out of my mouth faster than most of my jabs.

"Mancini, let the poor boy go. You're making a mockery out of yourself."

This makes the man named Mancini squeeze my neck harder. I refuse to slouch in pain, fighting harder, only to miss him each time. "No one disrespects me." Mancini's words sound like they're caught on a growl as he seethes at me.

It's unclear if he's talking to me or the other guy. My eyes dart around, finding the street is bare. The shops have shut their doors and now have Closed signs on them. Nothing about this is our normal steal. Out of nowhere, my two friends are being dragged toward us. Fear clouds their eyes as their feet drag across the pavement with the goons pulling them.

"Are you a coward who can't do his own dirty work?" Scott yells, fighting the grasp the men have on him.

"It's small dick syndrome," Jay yells out to Scott. He's stopped fighting the man holding onto him. I admire how he's always brave, never afraid to mouth off. "I bet they all suck each other."

Mancini raises his gun and shoots Jay without warning. I've never seen someone die in front of me before. I want to scream and fight, but I force myself to stay still.

"I didn't realize you're in the business of killing children," the second man says calmly but dripping with coldness. Scott and I are ignored while the men talk. The other man's posture is relaxed as he places his hands in his pockets. He shows no expression that he cares about my dead friend. A grin teases his mouth, confirming he rather enjoys provoking his friend.

"Rossi, your four daughters make you weak," Mancini sneers, making it sound like a threat, even though he didn't threaten anything in particular.

I watch Scott fight harder, fearful of the same fate. Without mercy, Mancini lifts his gun and shoots him too. I want to vomit, but I haven't eaten in three days. This time, when the other man takes his gun out, so does everyone else. The safety on the guns sound like dominos as they fall.

"Leave my territory. Our meeting is over." Rossi's commanding voice vibrates around me, and I watch Mancini eye me like I'm a bug he would love to kill.

My shoulders tighten, scanning for an escape path if I need it. My eyes blink more than they should as they ping-pong between the men. Rossi is not a man to be crossed. Fear slithers deep into my bones until the sensation is overwhelming.

"You pull that trigger again, and I will put you down," says Rossi.

"You're choosing a homeless kid over our alliance?" He's staring at me, the spit from his words hitting my face in a splatter. Disgust is written all over him as he returns his gaze to the one person who might be saving my life.

"I cannot approve of a marriage for my daughter to the son of a child killer. It has nothing to do with the boy." He laughs like someone told a joke.

My eyes continue to bounce between them while contemplating if I should try to slip away. Rossi places his heavy hand on my shoulder as if reading my thoughts.

"Then give him to me as a symbol of friendship." Mancini's wicked smile chills me, and I silently plead not to be given to him. For certain, it would mean death.

"I don't want your friendship. We are done here." My savior grips my shoulders, but I refuse to show pain. I don't think it's his intention, but rather he doesn't realize his strength.

"This is the beginning of the war." Mancini points his finger at Rossi, who doesn't seem shaken. He refuses to dignify the threat with a response, so I stand up taller, trying to mimic his stance.

Chapter 2

Luca Age 21

MY HEART HUMS ITS constant beat that acts as a calming lullaby. My face stays stoic with my signature slight grin, not wanting anyone to be able to read me. Even with no one around, I keep up the appearance, because someone is always watching. The sky has eyes and ears everywhere. There is a reason why they call me Luca "Smiley" Rossi. I've heard people say that catching my smile while being looked in the eyes is a sign of death. I've never thought much about it. Never had a reason to bluff, I suppose. When your father is one of the most important mob bosses around, you have bigger things to deal with.

I push the man in front of me, causing him to trip on his feet. My hand hooks into his collar before he falls, hauling him upright. His shirt's fabric rips, and he coughs from the weak hold it has around his neck.

Killing in broad daylight on a main street is how I prefer to take people out. I like the fear it instills in people. There's no need for secretive cleanup, because it sends the message loud and clear. Killing up close makes it less of a sport and it's too savage for my enjoyment. But it will be something I'm going to have to get used to. After all, I'm Nicoli Rossi's only son and the oldest of his children. But that doesn't make my four sisters weak. All of us kids were brought up similarly. Even the mafia needs an heir and a spare. My four sisters are the spares, in case something ever happens to me.

The abandoned oil refinery looms in front of me. It's busted-out windows with plywood coverings give the illusion it's vacant. What you don't see is the metal reinforcement inside that makes it bulletproof, nor the extra details, which prevents screams from being heard on the outside.

The massive building blends in with all the other out of date structures in the area. The area reminds me of a graveyard, each building another tombstone. Even the air has this rotting smell to it that never leaves, no matter the season. The area gives off this eerie vibe that if you stay too long, you will be trapped in this ominous loop from which, there is no escape.

If caught, a war will be brought down with its full wrath. These two families have been fighting since I came into the picture, which also happened to be the day Nicoli Rossi brought me home as one of his children. There was no discussion. He read me the rules and told me that if I disobeyed him, he would bury me himself. Afterward, he walked me into his home and introduced me to the rest of the family. Unlike everyone else, he gave me respect, and in turn, he gained my respect.

The man in front of me harassed my sister. He catcalled her like a common whore, calling her names and tried to touch her when she clearly wanted nothing to do with him. He's one of Mancini's men. Anyone under his control is deemed my enemy and our family's, but his actions led to this.

I have zero-tolerance for arrogant shits who think they can bother my sisters. Killing him in the building that Mancini uses for his killings will send a message.

One day, I'll be taking over. I'm the heir who gets to continue my family's legacy. I need the men to respect me and to believe I have no fear. Respect is the most important thing to me. I have killed for it. There isn't much I wouldn't do for it.

I've come with no backup, which is stupid as hell. But the chance of being caught on my own is lower than if I had others with me. I have to take my chances. The thought of being seen does nothing to get my heart pumping, unlike the adrenaline right before a shot. I'm the perfect marksmen. My father learned early on that I wouldn't become a family doctor or lawyer, or a politician. I much preferred to practice my aim and learn how to disassemble and reassemble his guns.

But that doesn't mean I can't have a cover job. My father still wants politics to be an option. All I need to do is keep my nose clean and stay out of jail. It's really out of my hands, so I keep on going as I please until the day comes I no longer have a choice.

The man in front of me doesn't try to beg for his life. He walks with his head up, with pride. The Mancini family is as powerful as mine. We both hold the largest territories, with the most loyal members. Even this guy won't snitch.

Coming to the main doors, I push his shoulders to turn him to me. "Kneel," I command.

He refuses, just as I expected. His kneeling wouldn't have changed his fate. But it gives me an understanding of how loyal he is.

Bringing my handgun out, I take a step back. I don't want his blood splattered on me.

"Last chance to kneel before your true king," I say, trying to mess with him. I don't enjoy torturing; it bores me.

He tilts his head higher.

Taking another step back, I hold up my gun. It's steady in my hand, even with the blood rushing through my body. It takes one shot, and he falls to the ground. Placing my gun behind my back, I wait to hear any sounds that are not mine. The sound of traffic is in the distance, but not any louder or different from any other day.

Stepping away, I turn and notice a girl walking down the street. Her feet have stopped and her head is tilted toward the evening sky. Not a single bird has made a sound since the bullet left the chamber of my gun as if scared to move.

I watch as she starts walking again at an awkward pace. I consider if I should kill her from here. I could do it easily. She glances over her shoulder, her face clean of makeup, making her appear young. There is no doubt she's much younger than me. She seems to be about the age of my youngest sister, who just became a teen.

Her dark hair is raven-like, in a simple ponytail. Her eyes are wide, shining with innocence. She's wearing a skirt and a sweater that's one size too large for her petite frame. Her glasses are three times the size of her already wide eyes.

I'm intrigued by why a girl like her would be walking alone around this side of town. Staying in the shadows, I follow her, much like a wolf. Staying in the dark edges, I almost laugh, watching her react with awareness that she's being followed but still not trusting her gut.

CHAPTER 3

ALY AGE 16

I 'M LATE ONCE AGAIN. My phone died, and I didn't realize the library's clock was twenty minutes behind. I knew I should have studied before my shift at the diner where my mom and I work. I've been told to stay away from the alleyway that holds the old oil refinery, which no longer runs.

This part of town has been forgotten, while everywhere else continued to grow and expand, staying in perfect upkeep. The streets might be vacant, but even if they weren't, no one would do anything. This side of town is where you don't make eye contact with people you pass on the street. Where no one sees or hears a thing. People disappear on this side of the tracks.

The sun has lowered close to the horizon, casting shadows in the street. Each shadow moves unnaturally, reminding me of spirits that need to tell their stories. My body rolls with a sudden shiver that runs through me. Walking the streets alone creeps me out, but I had no choice today.

A gunshot echoes in the vacant cracked streets. I stop, my heart in my throat, waiting to see if more come. I should have never taken the shortcut. Turning in a full circle, I see there's no one there. I begin to move my feet faster, wanting to get away from here, needing to get to work.

My feet go as fast as possible without breaking into a run. My glasses begin to shuffle down my nose at my ungraceful attempt to move faster. I'm no athlete. I've been described more as the bookish type.

My two left feet hit a lip in the cracked concrete, and I fall to the ground, cutting my hands and knees. A hiss escapes through my teeth as I glance around to see if anyone saw me. Shaking my head, I have to remind myself I'm the only person stupid enough to be back here, instead of taking the 'normal' way.

Just as I stand up, brushing away the dirt on my scraped knees, a dark figure appears. My skin prickles all of a sudden, and my heart picks up at an alarming rate. Squinting, I see a black hoodie framing the brightest blue eyes I've ever seen. They're incredibly vibrant, making me believe they must be contacts. I've never seen this guy around, telling me he shouldn't be here either. He steps toward me, an evil grin on his face as I watch him lift his fingers in a pretend gun-like fashion and make a subtle movement mimicking him shooting me.

My jaw drops with his action, but I stay standing and stare right into his eyes. Rationally, my mind is screaming at me to escape the alley as fast as possible, but my feet stay planted. I'm used to being ignored, and this is a blatant threat. I'm uncertain of what to do. I stand frozen as my mind spins at a thousand miles per hour. It takes me too long to come up with a comeback, and by then, a blacked-out town car comes down the road.

The figure dashes away, making me laugh. Coward.

The car begins to slow, but I keep walking, my head straight ahead. It trails me for a couple of yards before the window starts to crawl down. I can't escape this. It makes it harder for my mother when I become difficult.

"Daughter."

"Father," my voice squeaks, making me sound like a timid mouse.

Pierre Mancini is a scary man. He's the reason why no one bugs me, ever. Not even to be friends with me. Everyone is afraid to be around me for too long. I'm not one of his chosen children. I'm shoved into the shadows, because he has a wife who's not my mother. But in his controlling way, he keeps me safe. All while pretending I don't exist.

I recognize Jonny Mancini right away as he steps out through the back door. He walks over to me, and I watch our father nod. I know the drill. Jonny is to walk me to wherever I'm going. He mumbles, "Sins of my father." I'm used to him complaining as soon as our father is out of earshot. He thinks he's being punished for his father's sins by making sure I'm safe.

I continue walking, Jonny keeping stride with me. No words are exchanged. Not even when the diner comes into view. Without saying goodbye, I walk into the building, while Jonny takes a seat on the bench, pulling out a smoke. He won't linger, hating to be seen with me. I get it. I'm a reminder of what his father did. Even at that, the mafia's Italians have strong family values. The men may have a mistress or two on the side, but creating offspring with them isn't well received. We may be protected, but we're also shunned by those same protectors. Whether I like it or not, I'm a part of them, even if I'm outside their inner circle.

Entering the diner, I'm aware my mother's eyes are on me. I try to keep mine aimed down at the floor, but as I fasten the diner's apron, they come up and meet hers. She gives me a wary frown before a weak smile.

My mother has darker circles under her eyes compared to normal. She's been working double shifts each day this week, and she shows no signs of stopping. My mother is stubbornly wanting to save for my university instead of allowing my father to help. She believes his money is dirty and puts us under his control. Her moss-green eyes go to Jonny, then to me, which means she's aware I saw my father.

"Why were you late, honey?" She kisses the top of my head.

"I lost track of time while studying," I say honestly.

She lifts one eyebrow, questioning my answer without saying anything. Even my mother won't push me too far, being scared of my father. If I were to tell him I didn't want to live with my mom, I would be ripped away from her.

"You're a good girl. Just don't forget that." That is always what she says, afraid one day I will be welcomed into their world. Even though she's never admitted it, I know it scares her. My mother is my best friend, and I see how hard she works. I would never do anything to make her disappointed in me.

"I'm working hard to get us out of here, to make something of myself." That's my goal in life. Study hard, work harder, and get a high-paying job that will allow me to take us away from here. Somewhere that doesn't experience the wrath of the Mancini name. Somewhere we can blend in with the crowd. Make friends without them fearing my last name.

A large group is sitting in my section, and I head toward them to take their drink order. From the time I walk in, the rush starts, and it doesn't stop. I can't help but keep an eye on my mom. She has become slower lately, and I try to pick up the slack to help her.

I watch as a group of her former friends come in and are seated in her section. I go greet them before my mom even has a chance. These ladies used to be my mom's best friends before I came into the picture. Now, they snub her, pretending they were never close. I can see the hurt in her eyes every time. All because of me. Because I was born with the wrong father.

Leaving their table, a chill wraps around me. Peering toward the bench Jonny was on earlier, I see it's filled with teenagers. In fact, they're kids from my biology class. They all have smiles as they move around each other, laughing. Taking another glance around, I don't see anyone who doesn't belong. I have that sixth sense that I'm being watched. This is normally how I can tell if Jonny is around, or one of my father's minions.

Bustling back to the counter, I ring in the order, but the prickling awareness remains. Rubbing the back of my neck, I try to shove the agitation down. If my father needs me, I'll be summoned. No use being distracted while I work. Soon enough, I forget about the slight ping of tingles from being watched, and it fades away before my shift ends.

CHAPTER 4

LUCA

I'VE BEEN SEEN. MY feet freeze instantly as I assess the situation. There is a slight breeze, and I catch the scent of her light perfume. Instead of dread and failure consuming me, my senses are heightened, and I'm lighter on my feet. Pure excitement similar to the buzz I get before I press the trigger invades me.

Lifting my fingers into a mock gun I move them as if I've shot her. I expect her to run, or scream but she holds herself upright and stares at me harder. Casting my eyes over her, I see she is a stereotypical nerd. Nothing to be worried about. I slip out of her view but stay close, needing to ensure my instincts are correct. The girl seems innocent enough but also the type who would run to the cops. I can smell her fear. What is a girl like her doing back here? It intrigues me enough to stick around longer than I should.

A sleek black car with tinted windows appears, and she keeps walking like she's on any other street. The only people brave enough to be in this area are gangsters. The car stops in front of her, and she shrivels into herself. Interesting. I can't hear the exchange of words but recognize Jonny Mancini. He's my age. Mean motherfucker. Smart too. I have to admit my interest is piqued. What would they want with a girl like her?

I can understand the draw of her innocence, but she's too young to be a whore. Maybe age doesn't matter to them. Killing children never was a problem. I find myself preparing to defend her honor. Men who try to take advantage of women are scum. A real man should never have to force himself on someone to get laid. Being in the mafia is like a big shiny badge that says **Fuck Me**, and everyone listens. There is never a shortage of women who want to get under one of us.

Jonny doesn't seem interested in her. His scowl stays permanently painted on his face as he walks beside her. I take a quick photo, hoping I can get some type of ID on the girl. She's important enough to be escorted by a Mancini.

* * *

I find myself back in front of the diner, changed, free of any evidence I just murdered someone in cold blood. I'm pushing my luck being in Mancini territory, but I've never been one to follow rules.

As I push the door open, a bell rings above my head. I scan over the diner before I see a vacant booth off to the side. It'll give me a decent view while staying in the back.

"I'll be right with you, handsome," an older lady greets me with a warm smile.

I have to give the girl some credit. Her back straightens as soon as my eyes land on her. She goes to the large window and peeks out. Wrong way. For the briefest moment, I watch her get spooked, and I thrive on it. But then she squares her shoulders, pushing them back, and walks to her next table. I can see her slight twitches in recognizing someone has their eyes on her, but she never allows it to stop her.

The diner is out of date and below someone who would be tied to the Mancini family. Pierre is a cocky bastard, and nothing of his would be caught in a rundown place like this. Who is this girl?

Her movements are graceful, and she talks easily to all her tables. For a young girl, she is beautiful in that "I need to grow into myself" type of way. I see the way everyone is nice to her, adding to the conversations around her, but when she walks away, the whispers start. It's almost as if they are afraid to be rude to her but don't accept her as one of their own.

The older woman brings me my drink, hamburger, and fries. It takes me a minute of talking to her, when finally the resemblance between her and my mystery girl starts to take root. The way they interact together confirms my suspicion. They must be mother and daughter.

I leave a bit of a tip, but not big enough to be remembered clearly. When the older lady leaves, she's slow and has a slight limp to her step. She goes the way of the dim lamp posts, then down a dark walkway cutting through a park. The wind has picked up from this afternoon, pushing and throwing her hair, even though it's pulled back in a ponytail. My steps match hers as I stay behind. She never notices me, unlike her daughter. I plan to learn everything about this girl. She's important to Pierre Mancini, which means she's important to me. I have never forgotten the way he killed my two best friends without any mercy. One day, I plan to return the favor, to show him the same fate.

His people are always encroaching on our territory, trying to mark us as weak. My father, Nicoli Rossi, is a smart man— smarter than Mancini. We need to stay ahead of them; otherwise, they will attempt to ruin us to the best of their ability.

CHAPTER 5

ALY

I SENT MY MOM home once the rush died down. She became clumsier as the night progressed, dropping two plates that will cost her part of her paycheck. Her multiple sclerosis diagnosis weighs heavily on my mind, but she refuses to acknowledge it. She has dark bags under her eyes, even with all the concealer she wears. My mom is beautiful, but her hard life is starting to show.

The scattered streetlamps leave the empty street dim. It's just past midnight, and I enjoy the quiet walk alone. I'm not bothered by walking in the dark. Something about the night relaxes me; maybe it's the fact that I can easily blend in. With each step that takes me closer to home, my feet cry out in pain, wanting to feel that instant relief of not holding me up.

As a black town car idles around the corner, the soles of my feet pinch harder. Stopping, I lift one foot, giving it the release it needs. Placing it back down, the ache becomes worse than before.

My father steps out of the car, his wide stance intimidating. He's an attractive man, his hair jet-black with the sides slightly peppered with gray. He never smiles, his facial features chiseled and rough.

My lips purse as I wait for the reason I'm seeing him twice in one day. "Get in."

I jump at his deep, angry-sounding voice and nod, slipping past him. People consider me weak because I'm quiet. I'm not. I'm always thinking, calculating. I use my personality against others. The best thing about me is that I can slip in and out without being noticed.

The tension is thick in the air. This must be important for him to come himself and not send one of his men. We stop in front of his family's mansion. My heart pauses momentarily. I've never been inside before. It's not like I'm invited to his family gatherings. I'm meant to be the forgotten mistake of his past.

"Why am I here?" I ask, my voice strong.

He doesn't answer me but steps out, holding the door open for me to follow him.

Obeying, I begin to walk, my eyes darting everywhere, storing the information for later. The house is large, its main foyer bigger than the house I live in. Some of my father's bodyguards trail behind us, making me wonder where they came from.

He leads me down some stairs, the door closing with a latching sound. I refuse to check over my shoulder to see if I'm locked in here. My half-brother and his cousins come into view as I reach the bottom of the stairway. I've memorized all their names and have managed to figure out most of their ranks too.

I'm led to a floral chair that should be placed in a living room. It sticks out down here in the cold and uninviting basement. The floor is concrete, with patches of stains from things I don't want to think about. I guess the concrete makes for an easier cleaning job.

"What were you doing by the refinery?" Jonny asks, standing up.

I glance toward Father, trying to gather who's in charge. "Answer his question," my father tells me. Each day, Jonny is training and getting more responsibility to take over from our dad.

I may appear scared, but I'm not. "I was late for my shift, so I took the shortcut." I shrug.

Just when they think I'm done talking, I continue, because I would like to get out of here faster. "I take it the gunshot I heard was not one of yours?"

Instantly, I think of the bright blue eyes. He has some balls doing a blatant stunt like that.

I watch Hugo, my father's right-hand man, nod to a cousin, and then a lineup of men comes before me. I take each one in, shocked that those eyes aren't in front of me.

"Recognize any of these guys?" Jonny asks me.

Because I'm annoyed, I'm up past my bedtime and in a house I've never stepped foot in, or maybe because my ego has been hurt with them bringing me here because they need me, I refuse to give them the answer they're searching for. I give them my smart-ass response without them even realizing it. I have seen each man before, and I dictate the last place I saw each of them. All while never letting on that I saw someone else.

I'M DROPPED OFF AT my door once they realize I'm useless to them. Thrown away once again. Twisting the handle, I discover it's unlocked—like every time I come home later than my mother. She fell asleep on the couch, trying to wait up for me. She must have dozed off as soon as she came home, not realizing I'm home two hours later than I should be coming in.

I don't bother locking the door behind me. The thought doesn't even enter my mind. No one messes with us. And maybe it's our silent way of testing our limits. I cover my mom with a blanket and kiss her on her cheek before heading for my room.

My hand goes to flick on the light. It clicks, but I stay immersed in darkness. Must be burned out. Walking deeper into my room, I hear the crunch of another step that's in time with mine. Twisting a fraction, I feel a hand cover my face, muffling the scream that tries to escape, all while immobilizing me.

"Little birds need to have their wings clipped when they go where they shouldn't," the rough voice says into my ear.

Instantly, I know it's him. The blue-eyed man. He smells like metal and a crisp soap scent. His fingers are calloused as they splay across my face. His heat radiates off him in waves. I refuse to shiver from the fear coursing through me. I wait for him to break my neck or bring his gun out. When he does neither, I kick my leg out behind me. Simultaneously, I bite down on his hand, jerking out of his hold. When I was ten, Jonny was forced to give me self-defense lessons just in case. He bitched about it the whole time.

Instead of running out of the room, I go to sit on my bed, my feet welcoming the lightness as I take off my shoes. Bringing one foot up, I press my thumb deep into my arch, then repeat the process on my other foot. Out the corner of my eye, I can see his shock as he glares down at me with a furious intensity in his eyes. He doesn't make a move to come closer to me as he tries to read the situation.

"I could have you killed with one button pressed on my phone," I taunt without raising my eyes to him. I have no idea if it's true, but it sounds like it's something everyone in this town believes.

"I could have you killed right there on your bed," he counters, and this time, I meet his eyes.

Touché.

The way his eyes watch me is unnerving. Mocking his glare, I lift one eyebrow, daring him to make a move. My heart bobs, sitting in my throat, as I try not to get panicky in front of him. Instead, I keep my eyes narrowed to try to come across inconvenienced.

"Why didn't you give me up?" he asks with curiosity rather than anger. With the way his eyes are narrowed at me, there is no question he hates me—or at least what I represent.

Welcome to the club.

I smile back at him, giving in to the conversation. "Who said I didn't and you walked right into a trap?" I enjoy the way his right eye twitches, giving away his small sign of annoyance with me. He removes the hood from his head, showing me a clear view of his face. My breath whooshes out of me. He's handsome—like sexy movie star handsome. I was expecting some hoodlum with scars, but he resembles a model on a magazine cover.

He has blond hair that he has to use his fingers to move from his eyes. He has high cheekbones, plump lips. His shoulders are large and broad. I have no doubt under that big sweater is an expanse of muscles.

He stalks toward me until his boots are under my bed and his legs hit my bent knees. "Consider yourself under my protection now."

My eyes narrow on him, wondering what his angle is. If he wanted to get to my father through me, I would be dead by now. It makes me realize that maybe my father had a point all those times he made Jonny be my personal bodyguard.

"Trust me, I don't need protection. That's all people do around me." I inspect my fingernails, trying to brush off this new excitement. My heart flutters, and I flush under his watch.

"There will come a day." His hand reaches out and touches my dark hair before immediately dropping it like it stung him.

If caught, I contributed to my death by allowing him into my life. But like everything else, no one was around to witness it. My mother always said I should be an artist to free my imagination. I run with this new idealism of this blue-eyed man. For once in my life, someone sees me for me.

I allow myself to cling to that fantasy, even if it's all in my head.

Chapter 6

Aly Age 18

STANDING ON THE EDGE of the property, I eye the loud house party that is bursting with random people. I don't do people well. I avoid parties like the plague. I'm here because Jonny dragged me along with him. He grabbed me from walking home from work, because it was deemed unsafe to walk alone. But now, I'm still in the dark and alone, just at another location. Our father definitely didn't have this in mind when he sent Jonny to me.

I debate if I should continue to stand here outside his car or if I should start walking home. He said he would be a minute, as I watched him shove a gun into his side holster under his jacket. Jonny doesn't just carry one gun, and I'm nervous about why he felt he needed an extra above his two.

This is what I hate. The alpha dominance he thinks he has. What every mafia man thinks he has. It's the kill or be killed attitude when things don't go their way. I want nothing to do with it all. I want to study and make high grades. That is how you get out of this world. I refuse help, because it always comes with strings. Strings that will tie me and my mother here longer than I want.

"Aly Mancini, the lost princess," a guy from school says, walking up to me. He's been hanging around Jonny and his crew.

I'm conscious of the dark we're standing in right now. Cars line the area, but everyone is inside. I should have gone into the house with Jonny. No, I should have stayed in the car and locked the doors. Better yet, I should have stolen the car and taken myself home.

"How is it you've been left here by yourself?" He checks around before grinning at me.

"Jonny will be back any second."

He glances to the house, then back at me. "Naw. Rumor is his girl is fucking someone else in there. Jonny likes to take his time showing he's the boss. It'll be another hour 'til he's back. I'll keep you company 'til he returns. The dark isn't a place for a pretty girl like you."

My chest tightens, not liking how he's staring at me. He comes right up to me, his hand playing with the loose piece of hair that fell out of my messy bun. It probably is a mess, since I have two pencils keeping my hair up in place.

I want to step back but don't want him to know I'm nervous. With how he's checking me out, he would thrive on my insecurity. I'm uncomfortable, my body screaming on the inside.

His other hand comes up, making me flinch, even though I tell myself not to. He chuckles, taking the pencils out of my hair one at a time. My hair softly falls past my shoulders, with kinks that make it seem like I attempted to curl it, which I didn't.

"On another thought, maybe the dark is the perfect place for us," he rasps, his nose grazing my ear.

"I think I see Jonny." I step back, bumping into the car behind me. My eyes search the darkness, hoping for anyone I recognize. My spine stiffens as I realize no one would notice if I screamed. No one would notice I'm gone.

"Don't worry. I'll take good care of you while we wait. No need to be shy. I see the way you watch guys like me. I'll give it to you as good as you give."

My heart stills. I want to scream for help, but it's like I've forgotten how to open my mouth. White-hot fear digs its way further into my core, making my body tremble.

"Get the fuck away from her," a deep voice orders in a harsh tone—one I learned a couple of years ago belongs to Luca Rossi.

My heart pounds faster. He shouldn't be in our territory; the repercussions could get him killed. With the pounding in my chest, it warms my heart that he's here and is saving me. The tug of war on my heart and mind is constant when I'm in his presence. Since the moment we met when I was sixteen, he's popped into my life when I least expect him. Maybe that's why I stayed outside, hoping to see him again. I shouldn't have thoughts like this. He's the enemy. Jonny wouldn't think twice about killing him here in front of me.

The guy takes a step back to turn to our intruder. "This doesn't concern you. Leave us."

I hear the click of the gun before I can see it. "If you don't step away, I will shoot off your dick. If you so much as look at Aly again, I will cut your dick off while you sleep."

"With so much dick talk, it sounds like you're coming on to me. I'm not interested. Now go, before I find out who you are." Both guys stand strong, testosterone escalating each second that passes.

For a moment, the other guy stands tall, not backing down. I watch Luca, his fingers dancing up and down, reminding me of how they would move over piano keys. They're itching to grab his gun, wanting a reason to use it. The strange warm sentiment from him being here to protect me runs through my body. I should hate him, but I don't. He's mean and intolerable, yet kind and gentle with me. It's like my mind can't decide what he is.

Luca moves his jacket, showing his gun. His hand rests on it, daring the guy to match his move. The coward scoffs, turning to go into the party, leaving me alone with Luca. Our eyes connect for several seconds. His body is stiff, his brow arched as he glares at me. His lips are scrunched, leaving a little opening that allows for short breaths. His thumb absently brushes the black metal of the gun in what could be an attempt to calm his anger before he speaks.

My heart beats its typical strong rhythm in his presence, but not because I'm frightened. It's entirely from the way he's watching me.

"Are you trying to cause trouble?" he berates me, his gun moving to scratch the side of his head.

"Me? I was minding my own business."

He scoffs, his ocean eyes moving up and down my body. "Maybe if you stopped wearing those skirts, he wouldn't have wanted to fuck you."

My skirt goes past my knees. Double-checking, my hands slide down, searching for the hem. I have to arch to the side slightly, and my fingers still can't feel it. Yup, past my knees.

"My skirt is hardly the reason."

His presence is starting to annoy me as he takes on this "I'm better than you" tone. He steps into me, grabbing hold of my long black hair. "This hair is too much. It reminds men that they can hold onto it while they fuck you. The skirt is another reminder that all they need to do is bend you over. And those plump red lips makes them imagine what their cock would look like in your mouth." His reasoning is the most chauvinistic answer of mankind.

"Are you talking about men in general, or you?"

"Trust me, you don't do it for me. I see the way you lick your lips for my attention. I would have had you already if I wanted."

Luca is the most irritating, self-centered man I have ever met. My hand itches to slap him, wanting to see how he would react.

"Don't even think about it, little bird." That nickname drives me crazy every time he uses it.

"Now, be a good girl. I don't want to have to come back to save you." He starts to step backward, his eyes never leaving mine. They're intimidating and intense; the whole time, I have to fight to keep his gaze. The need to shy away digs into me, but I refuse. When the darkness has erased his whole figure, I'm able to breathe a bit easier.

"Aly, what are you doing out here?" Coy asks, walking up to me. "Did Jonny leave you?"

His forehead pinches before he glances at me then around, as if expecting Jonny to appear any moment. There is a tightness in his eyes like he's holding back from saying something. Or maybe he realizes he would be equally to blame from my father if something happened to me.

"He went in there with a gun," I say, unsure if I want Coy to go in to back him up.

"Let me take you home. This isn't your scene." He smiles at me, and I become shy from his comment. He's right; it's not. But I still hate that people assume that. Or maybe it's because they sound like they're judging me for it. I can't tell which one. But Coy is safe. He's been around as long as Jonny. His father is one of my father's top men.

"Thanks, Coy," I say, checking behind me to see if I can spot Luca. He's long gone, leaving me to wonder why he was here anyway. With each step I take away from the party, my heart slows to a regular beat.

Chapter 7

Aly Age 21

FINISHING UP MY LAST appointment of the day, I drag my fingers through my perfectly combed dark hair while sitting back. The girl I interviewed is younger than I normally take on, fresh-faced, pouty lips, but haunted eyes. Hearing her heart-wrenching story, I didn't have it in me to turn her way. How could I, when she's had a hundred times the life experience I have, and a year younger. Up until this time, I have always made sure the girls were twenty-one. That age makes everything easier. They can go anywhere with my clients, they're mature enough with life experience, and I'm certain they understand what they're getting into. If I thought for a second they couldn't cut it or didn't understand the full impact of what they were signing up for, I'd never accept them.

I'm not your typical madam. My whole business started innocently enough, as a matchmaker. But as I talked to people and started to crunch the numbers, being a badass female pimp seemed like a better fit. It gave me the whole "living on the edge" vibe. If I were to ask a professional, I bet they would say it's an attention-seeking activity, to see what I can get away with under my father's nose. The truth is, I needed money, and being a madam brought that in instantly. It wasn't until after I realized I love what I do. I made a community that I became important in.

My phone rings, drawing me from my thoughts. I answer in my usual pseudo yoga studio salutation, but like many times before, all I hear is static. I've had two girls come to me believing they've been followed, but nothing has happened. The whole thing is creepy, but no one has taken any action. It might be a scare tactic, but I don't understand why. Discretion is mandatory, and I'm the best this city has. It's why politicians use me, why married men come to me for help. All my girls' identities are secret, keeping both parties void of risk. It helps that they have that girl-next-door look, with a hint of extravagance. It makes it harder to stereotype who might be in the business.

My clients are always satisfied, and this is one of the reasons I've become the top madam in Texas and the surrounding area. Hell, I sometimes have men asking me to fly my girls to them. My girls are all top-notch, and they get paid very well for it. They can afford to live in penthouses, buying expensive shit, because they've made a killing through me.

I have a growing empire at my fingertips. My father would be proud—if he knew about it. But then, like everyone else, I would have to pay my tribute.

My "yoga studio" is where I help train the girls in dancing, pole dancing, and any other skill they may require. Sometimes, it may be a piece of simple information on conversations that will be talked about, or to give them tips on how to fool the wives of my clients. I've seen everything, so I'm not shocked by any request. Casting my eyes over my studio, I ensure everything is in its place before I head out to lock up for the day.

I can sense him before he presses his chest to my back, his nose sliding down the side of my face. My so-called protector. "You need to be more careful. If I know what you're up to, so do others." My heart flutters like it always does when he's nearby. As much as we fight, I love having him around.

"I'm not your concern," I repeat for the thousandth time to him over the years.

"Little bird, you're not ready to spread your wings yet."

"I'm old enough to open my legs but not my wings?" I taunt him. He's never made a move on me before, yet he won't allow anyone else to either. I like getting him mad, reminding him that I'm all woman now. I'm no longer a young sixteen-year-old girl. It's the irrational part of me that allows my heart to get hurt when he's made it clear he doesn't want me that way. Why would he? He's part of a rival family. Our birthright is to hate each other, until death do us part. If I go down this rabbit hole, I'll end up confusing myself.

"Do you remember what happened last time you did?" His hand wraps around my belly, pulling me closer, his erection sticking into my back. It's sad it will go to waste, when it feels so strong.

"You beat him to a pulp. Jonny took credit for it after he found out who he was to me." My body stiffens, reminding me that I don't like him; I hate him. I have only ever had one boyfriend who was brave enough to seek me out. I couldn't even get fully naked before Luca beat him up. No one has ever made an effort after that, leaving me untouched.

"Jonny is a pussy. He's lucky I don't kill him." His lips graze my earlobe, but I refuse to melt into his hold.

"All talk, no action," I say, teasing him.

"I can take everything you have away. I suggest you don't piss me off, little bird." His voice is low, cold, and dripping with hate. I've never understood why he keeps visiting me, when he can hardly stand to be in my presence.

"Why must you call me a bird?" I question, annoyed he's bothering me.

"Because you're too young to see the cage around you."

"If you keep bothering me, I'll go to my father," I say sternly. I've never threatened this, but he's never threatened my livelihood, my business.

"No, you won't. You've waited too long. He'll see it as you playing with the enemy."

I spin around, but he still holds me. My breasts are rising and falling against his chest. A handful of people have seen my temper. I like to pretend to be meek, because I can get away with more. But he pushes me to my limits.

My eyes narrow on his bright blue ones. I'm no longer in awe of their color, because I've had to see them too many times. Pressing my hips impossibly close to him, I push against his dick. I want to prove my point that he's all bark and no bite. It's our weird telepathic way of having a silent conversation, all while having a different one out loud.

"There will come a day I'm more powerful than you. Then we will see who is really the bird," I say sweetly, smiling at him.

I'm not stupid. He would have killed me by now if that was the plan. As I see it, I have two of the most infamous mafia families watching out for me. I'm untouchable. I let them all believe they're pulling the strings, when in fact they do everything I want. They can keep calling me a silly girl, when the truth is, I'm smarter than them.

My phone rings between us, and he snakes his hand into my purse and pulls out my cell. His eyes turn cold, seeing Jonny's name on the screen.

"It's my brother." I try to grab my phone, but he keeps it above my head. I watch him decline the call. "That's going to bring him here. We Mancini's are stubborner than hell."

He grunts before he continues rifling through my purse. I hate this man in front of me. In fact, I think I hate all men. Every person in my life tries to control me in whatever way fits them best. Maybe that's why I've excelled at my job. I'm familiar with how they think, what they want, and allow them to believe they're getting exactly that.

I never want to be in a man's control, and because of that, I refuse to date. I'm always the bridesmaid and never the bride. I will walk through fire to not be someone else's property. Falling in love is a guaranteed way for me to lose my independence and to be muted forever. I would much rather set people up, watch them be happy for a night, and line my pockets with money.

Once he's done searching for whatever he thought he might find, he hands me back my purse.

"We should have a bet to see if you'll still be here by the time Jonny comes. My guess is a bullet to the heart immediately."

He glares down at me. Giving me the attention I thrive on, causing my heart to pound and creating a sensation that it wants to implode. I never understood this reaction to him.

"Shoo, run away," I taunt him more, even though I'm curious what would happen if they met.

"You disrespect me, and I will spank your skinny ass so hard your future children will feel it." His rough voice causes goose bumps to shiver down my body. He lifts a cocky eyebrow, all while his eyes stay hard and cold. I have no doubt he would spank me until my ass bled.

I try to rein in my frustrations and become the meek girl they all think they can control, while I begin to think about how I can get rid of him. I have no use for his protection. Not that I ever did. But I'm bored with this game we've been playing for years.

Chapter 8

Luca

ALY MANCINI CAUSES ME the most headaches in my life, and I'm a sniper. I want to strangle her with the way her dark-gray eyes challenge me, the way she sticks her nose up at my presence. All while my dick reminds me that I want to fuck the shit out of her. Every time I see her, I leave frustrated and angrier than when I appeared. She needs to be taught a lesson in gratitude. The problem is she has a chip on her shoulder and refuses to acknowledge what people have done for her.

I have to remind myself that the reason I keep her around and tolerate her shitty attitude is because she didn't rat me out all those years ago. There will also come a day that I'll need her. She will be her father's downfall. She is his weakness, and yet for a smart girl, she is blind to his affection.

War is coming, and she will be what protects me. I almost laugh that she actually believes I am her protector. Walking away, I don't go far. I have a mental countdown as to when Jonny appears to see if everything is okay with precious Aly. I watch him in competition with her, and it's fucking humorous. He competes with her for their father's attention. Each time he is forced to check in on her burns a hole of jealousy into him.

The fact that she thinks her side gig is invisible to the world shows how naïve she truly is. I'll give her props that she built this from the ground up all by herself. But there is a reason why her girls are safe and never had an issue before. Dear old Daddy and I would bust anyone open if they disrespected her or her business. When you have mafia who are willing to kill you if you wrong her, it's easier to be a gentleman.

"Why the hell did you not answer my phone call?" Jonny barges out of his car, his sweet soon-to-be bride, Milana, beside him. Interesting, my little bird interrupted their date.

He puts his hands on her and starts dragging her to the car. I have to bite the inside of my lower lip to not give him a piece of my mind. All in due time. I'll enjoy ruining their family.

I step away before I do something stupid like rip Jonny's hand off for touching what's mine and head back to my territory. I need to set up anyway. My body tingles with excitement, and I'm uncertain if it's from seeing Aly or the anticipation of shooting someone.

She's grown up well. No longer in her awkward teen years, and she's really embraced her inner sexy librarian persona. It's hotter than hell. My cock grows harder thinking about me sticking it in her mouth to shut her up. I can tell she's attracted to me but fights it every step of the way. She's falling into my plan perfectly. What would old Pierre Mancini say when he finds out his daughter has been crushing on the enemy for several years?

Checking my phone, I see everything is going as planned. Once again, the Mancinis have set up shop on our corner. Not just that, our last gun shipment was confiscated by an anonymous group. Funny how the Mancinis seem to have all my new guns.

CHAPTER 9

ALY

"I'M NOT A CHILD," I tell my brother, who grunts while holding me tightly. His fingers pinch into my skin as he maneuvers me where he wants.

"If you had picked up your phone, I wouldn't have to come get you, and now I'm late."

He pushes me into the back of the car. I don't think Jonny ever had a time where he wasn't upset over something. "Just drop me off at my house," I direct him.

"Who wears a pencil skirt and a silk blouse when doing yoga?" He eyes me suspiciously.

"I was doing paperwork." Crossing my arms, I refuse to meet his stare in the rear-view mirror.

"Well, you're going to have to come with us now. I don't have time to be late."

I had plans that consisted of a nice bottle of red wine, a bubble bath, and a certain book that was steamier than my bathroom. I hate that Luca's face pops up immediately as I think about being naked in the privacy of my home. Placing all my frustrations from Luca onto Jonny, I try to hit him where it hurts.

"You're just like our dad." Jonny hates it when I refer to Pierre Mancini as my dad. The actual comment, he's proud of. He wants to be our father in every way and admires him. My pure existence is a thorn in his side. And I wonder if it's because he's been tagged as my babysitter countless times throughout the years, or something else.

"You two do fight like siblings," his betrothed Milana says.

Jonny is not a nice man. He gives Milana the death glare, which even makes me stay quiet. The thing is, there are five years between Jonny and me, and more gaps between Jonny's two younger brothers and me. Altogether, there are three Mancini boys; the other two are twelve and seventeen. They're just now starting to be brought up into this world. I've seen them but haven't had any interaction with them. It's not like how Jonny and I have always been pushed together.

"Tell me, why did you turn down the business program?" My chest squeezes at his question. Jonny has made a lot of silent accusations. Maybe Luca was right and more people are aware of my illicit business. I wanted to go into accounting, but business was booming, the money too lucrative. If I left, I would be starting over from scratch. And to be honest, I've come around to living here.

It also doesn't help that I've had to place my mother into a home, with her multiple sclerosis becoming more aggressive. I've already had to accept my father's money to help me with that. Accepting his money to send me to school seemed wrong, when I knew it was against my mother's wishes.

I had to do something to make ends meet, and this is how I came up with my business.

"Hey, Jonny." I turn to see Coy jumping into the back of the car. He kisses me on both cheeks. "I take it you're my date, Aly."

I fight my eye roll. Disrespect is a big crime, and I don't have the energy to apologize for it tonight. Reverting to my silent, meek persona, I absently stare out the window. It's not that Coy is a bad guy; he's cute and has always been kind to me. But I can't misconstrue those as real qualities of being honorable or friendly. The quiet ones are always the worst.

Coy places his arm across the back seat, trying to be casual. Turning from the window, I lift my brow, causing him to laugh. "Relax, Aly, I don't bite." Bending closer to my ear so no one else can hear, he murmurs, "I'm stuck here just like you. We might as well enjoy ourselves."

That brings an unwanted smile to my lips, and he pokes me knowingly. I watch our territory limits disappear as we head into an area close to the Rossi family's land.

"Why are we here?" I ask.

"Coy and I need to take care of some business before we head out. Like I told you earlier, I didn't have time to be late."

My body freezes up, and I already know something is wrong. "Coy?" I'm unsure of what I'm asking. Jonny and Coy have been best friends growing up. Both are made men because of who their fathers are.

"You worried about me?" He winks. "I knew I liked you." He squeezes my shoulder. Lately, Coy has been around Jonny whenever I am. I have no doubt he's the type of man my mafia family would love to court me. Hell, maybe they've already had talks and this is the start of it.

Jonny interrupts him, "Stay here, girls."

Falling against the back seat, we resemble sitting ducks, and I'm not about to be some damsel in distress. I've been taking care of myself my whole life. The area is vacant, making my skin crawl. There should be people on the streets and children on the playground across the road.

We watch the men strut away full of confidence. They don't check over their shoulders, their postures relaxed. "We need to leave," I say under my breath, but it's clearly heard. I don't recognize the building as one of the family's. Jonny's typical bodyguards and men stand on the street. They're stiff, their eyes darting all around as they stand guard. The eerie tingle that shoots up my spine tells me something is wrong.

"Aly, I love you, but you need to learn to listen. Not listening will get you killed." Milana replies. I want to scream that maybe her dear old Jonny shouldn't bring her to a business deal before a date. It's bad manners and stupid.

"Listening is going to get you killed. I thought you wanted marriage and the whole happily ever after story. You're not going to get it if you're dead."

She scoffs, clearly not wanting to disobey Jonny.

I don't bother going into a tirade about why marriages are never a happily ever after anyway. But I have her on this point.

"I trust Jonny." Milana nods her head certain of him, refusing to question anything.

The men go into a storefront, and I step out of the car. Slipping off my four-inch heels, I walk barefoot across the street. The area is vacant, not a soul in sight. Dread coils inside of me, fearing this is a setup. If Luca let me answer my phone, I would be safe in my little apartment, on my way to being happily tipsy.

Gunshots are heard, my eyes opening wide. Last time I heard a gunshot was five years ago when I met Luca. I watch Jonny running out of the building toward the car. Milana is hysterically screaming, and moving around franticly. My eyes dart from the door to the car, waiting for Coy. Maybe I should have stayed in the vehicle after all. I'm about to rush back, when I'm tugged backward.

"What the hell are you doing here?" My body already recognizes it's Luca. He smells like gun powder, metal, and a hint of cinnamon.

"Let me go!" I try to knee him, but he's too smart for that, moving away from my favorite move.

Coy comes out of the building in no rush, flipping his gun around his fingers like this is everyday stuff. He's whistling as he struts toward the car. His feet stop, and I can hear him call my name. Our eyes meet, and he lifts his gun, pointing it at me—or Luca, but I'm the one in front.

Jonny turns the engine on, and I watch it all happen in slow motion. A bottle filled with what I'm assuming is gas and a cloth on fire is tossed into the car. Gunshots follow as Coy runs toward me. All hell breaks loose, the explosion and heat throwing me and Luca to the ground.

The back of my head hits the cement border of the kids' playground as I hear guns and yelling. A rough pain shoots up my arm just before strong arms lift me. I expect Luca to be cradling me, and I want to hug him.

My eyes flutter, trying to open, wanting to see his handsome face, only to realize his smell is all wrong. Forcing myself to focus, I peer up and see Coy, holding me in his steady grasp.

I can't help but search for Luca. He's nowhere to be found. Another car squeals up, and for each step, another of their guns is taken out. I wait to be killed in Coy's arms, but anyone who gets close is shot as he rushes for the back door of the car.

Jonny must have a sniper out here, is my last thought before the pain I felt earlier tears through my body, and a scream leaves me. My arm burns like it's on fire. I can smell burned flesh, causing me to go lightheaded before I feel blood seeping down me and onto Coy.

"Jonny?" I ask, remembering the explosion. Coy doesn't utter a word while keeping me in his arms even once we're in the car. He's yelling out instructions, and our bodies are slammed into the seat before he rips off his shirt, placing it on my arm.

In my heart, I know Jonny is dead. I'm unsure how to react to the thought. We fought, and I always said I didn't care for him. But the ache in my heart tells me otherwise. No matter what, he was my brother. The only sibling I knew and interacted with. Even though he hated it, I knew he would keep me safe.

Then, my heart does another nosedive.

The heir to the Mancini throne is gone.

CHAPTER 10

LUCA

ALY MANCINI IS GOING to get me buried six feet under. I willingly murdered my own blood and family, all to save her while she was cradled in another man's arms. I'm a traitor, but I killed more of their men than mine. My heart twists with disgrace littering my soul. My father has given me everything, and I do something reckless like this? My heart pounds, not getting the memo. It will always save Aly first. That's the fucked-up part. I'm so obsessed with using her for my revenge that I saved her instead of allowing Mancini to lose two children instead of one.

Sitting in a family meeting, we talk strategy for getting them back. I'm half paying attention. I need to find out if they have a target for me. The impulse to shoot something or someone makes me fidgety. I'm unnerved, a feeling that is uncommon for me.

"The Mancini family is out an heir, and the old man is scrambling. He thinks marrying off Aly Mancini to a made man will fix this. People recognize a real heir when they see one. No one will follow a girl he hasn't accepted as one of his." Uncle Tony says. There is laughter around the room at the thought of a female being a leader. I use my father's reaction to guide me on how to respond. I have four sisters, all of whom he treats equal to me.

My father's face is emotionless, his thoughts hidden away for himself.

"That's not true. He accepted her the moment he put protection on her, and now he's marrying her to one of his men. He's rebuilding," I toss out my opinion. Without a doubt, she is meaningful to him.

The men start murmuring amongst themselves, and I realize they're talking about her getting married. My heart constricts tighter, acting like a chain is locked around its hard beat, daring it to fight its way free. It's a similar sentiment I had when I saw a gun lined up with her, ready to shoot to kill.

"There is tension between the ranks. Let them fight amongst each other, weakening themselves. We don't want to give them a common enemy to unite them," my cousin Pauly says. It's a horrible idea, but I see some nods in agreement. Again, I watch for my father's reaction. I'm always trying to learn from him. From experience, I know he won't say a word until after he has taken in everyone's ideas, and then he'll give his final decision.

"When's the wedding?" I hear myself ask. I notice the way their faces change as ideas fill their minds. They want to go in blazing. And all I think about is saving her once again. She will never belong to anyone but me. She is mine to torture.

"A week after the funeral," someone answers me as I devise a plan to move ahead quickly.

I don't normally speak up in these things, but this needs to go down as I have planned for the last five years. "I have a better idea." I smile.

The room grows silent, all eyes shifting to me. My father gestures with his hand, indicating I have the floor.

I now have a way to use Aly. If we want a war, I'll bring them a war.

CHAPTER 11

ALY

I'M SAT DOWN IN my father's living room. This is the second time I've ever been in their house. My father has his head in his hands. I've never seen him like this.

"How is your mother?" he asks after an awkward amount of time has passed. He peers up at me, and I don't recognize the expression he gives me.

"Not good. Her speech has gone downhill rapidly. She complains she has a hard time sleeping."

He nods.

My mother was diagnosed with MS ten years ago. The last two years have been particularly bad. She now has to be in a wheelchair, and her condition keeps deteriorating. It's the most heartbreaking thing to watch. The woman who has loved me more than anything in life can no longer defend herself. She is reliant on everyone around her, something she never wanted.

His eyes are somber as he reaches for my hand. "Aly, Coy has asked for your hand."

My head jerks up, on edge more than before. My head is spinning with ways to get out of this. Ways my father will understand.

"It's a good match. He will treat you well." His rough hand rubs the top of mine. My mother will have a heart attack when she finds out. This is the one thing she didn't want for me. My father is trying to marry me off.

"Coy wants to marry me." It's a statement, not a question. I think all my intelligence went out the window as I was faced with marriage. A marriage I don't want. "I have no intention of getting married." My voice is hardly audible as I speak to my father. Never once has he pushed me in this direction; it's confusing.

"You are the rightful heir now, Aly. It's time people respect you for it. You can't hide your whole life. I've allowed you to live as free of the lifestyle as possible. It was the one wish your mother made, and it killed me to do it. But I can no longer keep that promise."

His statements swirl inside my head. "Just because I'm the heir doesn't mean I need to be married."

"My decision is final. You will be married a week from Saturday." He starts to stand up, ending the conversation.

"I won't," I rebuke, stronger, finding my backbone. "This isn't the old days where arranged marriages happen. I have a future, and I won't let you block it." My anger is stirring as I think of everything I will lose.

"You will!" my father yells, his voice bouncing off the walls, hitting me right in the gut. He's never raised his voice before, so it startles me. "Otherwise, the insignificant business you play around with will be gone. You're lucky I haven't stopped this before. I should have forced you to go to school, away from here, but I'm a selfish man. The time has come. You chose your spot when you didn't leave for college, and again when you chose your profession. You are a true Mancini." There is no room for argument, and I hear a hint of pride as he talks to me.

"No." I cross my arms over my chest as I hold my ground.

Father slaps the table beside him, his voice rising to a level I've never heard before. "You are. You will take your rightful place. End of discussion." He looms over me, looking every bit the dangerous gangster he is. This is what everyone else sees when they look at him. It's scary. He's acting like I'm one of his subordinates, not his daughter. I know better than to argue. If I refuse, I'll lose my business and every other freedom I have grown accustomed to.

"I would hate for your mother to have to experience grief like my wife currently is," he warns, and I have no doubt he just threatened my life. It chills me to the core the way he seethes at me and the way his beady eyes glare at me. This is the head of the Mancini family everyone is frightened of.

S INCE THE NIGHT I was told I would be married off, much like a cow is sold in an auction, I have been held prisoner in my father's house.

It's not that Coy is a terrible person. One day, we could probably grow to love each other. He's easy on the eyes, and I would be taken care of for the rest of my life. But I don't want that.

I don't like the confinement marriage signifies to me. I don't want to be someone's property. I don't want to answer to someone about my whereabouts, who I talk to, or anything else. I don't want someone to think they have control over my business.

Coy may seem kind and reasonable, but he is every part an alpha mafia man. There are roles, and I don't see him bending to my wants.

Picking up my brush, I comb through my hair gently as I watch myself in the mirror. Tomorrow, I will become a wife. Tomorrow, the life I've come to cherish ends.

"I always knew you were weak." Luca's voice comes from behind me, but I can't see his reflection in the mirror.

Spinning around, I search to find him by my open window. He has a lazy grin on his face, and his eyes sparkle. They are bright and vibrant, a shade I've never seen on him before.

"How did you get in here?" I ask, realizing I'm wearing a sheer nightgown. It hangs to my feet, but my body is not hidden from him.

Standing, I try not to worry about being on display for him.

"You're about to be married to the wrong man, and you're worried how I got in here?" He clicks his tongue, walking toward me. I watch his eyes search my confused face before they lower. My nipples strain, becoming puckered as his eyes continue down my body in their perusal. That lazy grin grows larger. "You truly are a caged bird. You didn't even fight it. I'm disappointed in you."

"All I have to do is scream, and I will have ten men rush in here holding guns."

"Then I would have to kill each and every one for seeing my bride in the state she's in. Their deaths would be placed onto your shoulders."

"Your bride? You're the enemy." I stammer, staring up at him, my heart pounding frantically. "I'm to marry Coy."

"Making you become a wife to the wrong man," he says coolly.

"I'm not marrying anyone," I say in one breath, but my words sound defeated. I'm walking down the aisle tomorrow, and there is nothing he or I can do about it.

"I thought you were marrying Coy." His brow rises, challenging me while keeping his relaxed state.

I'm becoming flustered with the way he's intently staring at me. My chest rises and falls rapidly, and I wish I had a plan.

He picks up my housecoat and tosses it to me. "Put this on. You need to walk to the back door."

"I'm not going anywhere with you," I grit out through my teeth.

"Don't play with me. I will kill you right here. Trust me, dear old daddy would rather there be a sinful vow than have to bury another child. He will see this soon enough."

Keeping my spine straight, I tell him, "No." The adrenaline rush has my blood pulsing through me at a hazardous pace.

Out of the corner of my eye, I see the jagged knife he's holding in his left hand. An evil smirk rests on his lips, as if asking, What are you going to do about it?

"You will learn to forgive me," he tells me.

My body twists to step away, but simultaneously, I feel a sharp poke at my neck.

"What have you done?" I manage to ask before I slump into his arms.

"I'm making sure you stay safe, little bird."

CHAPTER 12

LUCA

I 'M OUT OF THE Mancini estate before they realize I was in there. Aly is securely in my arms, sleeping peacefully. Her relaxed facial features remind me of how young she is. I'm five years older than her, but it seems like a lifetime ago I was twenty-one.

She is breathtaking with her dark hair against her pale skin. She reminds me of Snow White but with longer hair. Unlike the fairy tale, there will be no Prince Charming to wake her up with a kiss. I'm the closest thing to a friend, and I plan to use that leverage as much as possible. Finally, the Rossis will be able to take out the Mancinis.

Our two families are both ambitious, always stepping on one another's feet. Soon, the Mancinis will bow down to us and become our puppets to play with.

Coming to my family's compound, I order my men away to avoid them seeing what is mine. I don't leave her side, refusing to meet with the men while she lays unconscious. I don't trust anyone with her. After all, she is the daughter and future of the one family we hate. Even as I lie beside her in my bed in the dark, my gun rests in my hand. My eyes may be closed, but I hear everything. I've been trained to not need my eyes.

She begins to stir, and I sit up, not wanting to frighten her. Inch by inch, I ease myself into a standing position. I have no time to change, staying in my boxers. Her gray eyes shoot open, wide as ever. They don't flutter or close, instead staying locked on me.

"Good morning," I tell her, keeping my face hard and cold.

"Where am I?" she asks, confused. Her hand goes to her head with a moan. I have ibuprofen and water by the bed if she wants it.

I bring up my gun to scratch at my temple, liking how she sucks in a breath. "You are in my castle now, bride."

"I'm no one's bride."

There's that feistiness I've come to enjoy. Normally, I find strong women annoying and too obstinate. I like a woman who does as I say and doesn't give me lip back. But the way her lower lip pushes out makes me want to nip it. My cock hardens further from her arguing. There is no hiding it in my tight boxers.

I stare into her eyes, hoping she's taking me in. I want to see her reaction. But she never does as I want. Stubbornly, she meets my gaze, even as she sits up, the covers dropping around her hips.

"We'll see. Soon, you will come to like this cage better than your other one. I'll even open the door, and you won't leave me."

"I hate you," she seethes, sitting up straighter in the bed we shared. She winces, and I watch her internal fight as she tries to ignore the headache she must have.

"Don't say things you don't mean. It just makes me angry," I say coolly.

She's testing me. I love seeing her willpower and preserving nature. My eyes drift down just for a second to get a better view of what's mine. I'm hard as steel, seeing her in that sheer nightgown. It's beyond painful. But I refuse to give her the satisfaction of showing her I like what I see. Instead, I stare right into the depths of her soul, acting unaffected. She has always been mine, even if she never realized it.

From the first time I laid eyes on her, I knew I would have her one day. I won't make it easier on her. She needs to realize she's mine on her own. We were meant for each other.

Until then, I will treat her as the enemy. One that I will enjoy breaking in. No matter how many times I tell myself I'm doing this for the good of the family, my heart recognizes the lie.

"Get dressed. You have your wedding dress fitting in an hour," I command.

Her jaw tics at my demand. Her eyes narrow with hatred before a sinister smile takes the place of her frown. Holding my eyes, she lifts her nightgown over her head, leaving her completely naked in front of me. She stands up, her hands on her hips.

Blood rushes straight to my dick. If she were to stab me right now, I wouldn't even bleed. She is perfect in every sense. Her skin is unblemished, smooth, and soft-looking. Her tits are small but perky. I wonder what she'd look like bouncing on my cock. Seeing her fully naked, my body reacts like a thirteen-year-old boy seeing tits for the first time.

"What clothes do I wear?" she has the nerve to sass back at me.

I'm caught off guard by her. Words stop flowing in my head, and I have to swallow my saliva down. It takes every bit of my willpower not to take her here, right now.

Swiping my dress shirt from the floor, I toss it to her. I didn't think to get her clothes. With a knowing smirk, she pulls my shirt over her head. I watch her lick her bottom lip, and I can't wait until I see those lips wrapped around my cock.

"Better," I manage to say roughly. Now it seems to be her staring at my naked chest. "Like what you see?" I bring my hand to rub at my strained cock, wanting her to see what damage she's caused me. The air is thick between us.

"Don't flatter yourself." She rolls her eyes and laughs at me cockily like she's the one in power.

I push her back against the bed, leaning my whole body on her. Her sassy mouth might turn me on in here, but she needs to learn she can never do this in public. It will end up getting her punished, or worse, killed. Fear clouds those beautiful irises.

"Don't disrespect me." I push against her, my arousal pressing to her stomach. I want her to realize what she does to me. She squirms, making me harder with each movement.

"They'll come for me, and when they storm your castle, you'll regret this." She sounds so certain I feel bad for her. I refuse to lose.

I rub my nose up from her jaw to her forehead. "You're wrong. By the time you realize it, this will be your castle too."

Before I can think, I press my lips to hers. It's hard and bruising, yet soft upon her pouty lips. It takes a second for her to open up to me, a moan escaping her.

I break away, leaving her wanting more. I don't turn when I hear her gasp, already picturing her angry fumes dancing above her head. I head to the guest bedroom to grab a shower before I leave for the family meeting that's been called.

I walk in late, only because I'm not early. Everyone is sitting down at my father's dinner table like we would for a family dinner. My ma cooked up a storm, but her presence is no longer here.

Clapping erupts as I step farther in and the men take notice of me. My father stands, hugging me before placing a kiss on my forehead.

"I think it's time we make your son a made man," my uncle says, coming up to greet me and kissing me on the forehead. I wait to see if my father disputes it. He's all about me proving myself. Unlike the Mancini family. Jonny received his made-man title because of his birthright. They may have cooked up some event to help it go smoothly, but he was undeserving. I've been working my balls off for years to get recognition.

"How does she feel, boy?" another of my uncles asks, licking his lips like he wants a piece. An unexpected protectiveness has me clenching my fingers into a fist before I realize a move like this will be noticed. Uncurling my hands, I don't have time to comment, as some asshole shouts, "He's waiting for the wedding night," causing everyone to laugh.

"I don't care what the hell he does after we get an heir. He can send her body back home in a body bag for all I care," someone adds to the banter.

No one will be killing Aly but me. I survey the room, noticing several of the men watching me. This is a test.

"If anyone gets to feel her soft neck in their hands, it's me. I'm the one who decides when she's no longer useful."

I'm still fuming as they talk about taking her out as if it's no bigger deal than ordering a pizza. I almost miss the heir comment. That should be fun. Mancini will be forced to turn his back on his daughter, realizing she is one of us.

No one blinks an eye at the crude words. Normally, I wouldn't give a shit either. But it seems wrong to be talking about murdering Aly when we're planning our wedding. No matter the circumstances. It reminds me why I have never let myself grow close to anyone. I have no room for love. It was stupid to say I would marry her. It was an impulse, and a stupid one at that. She can be found as a weakness if I show her too much favoritism.

My anger grows at my stupidity. I have been trained to not jump to conclusions, to take my time and think things through. It's these skills that make me a damn great sniper. I'm always ten steps ahead of everyone.

CHAPTER 13

ALY

M Y DOOR BURSTS OPEN as two robust women with big smiles roll a bunch of white dresses on a clothing rack into the room.

"Well, aren't you a pretty one," one of them says warmly as she continues to bring the rack in.

"I've heard rumors of your beauty but didn't realize they did you no justice," the other one says, breezing by me, placing a wooden stool down along with other things she was carrying.

"Luca has always liked them pretty."

My heart stills hearing this. It's silly and irrational. They talk amongst themselves like I'm not here or the center of their conversation. I'm able to catch their names, Cecilia and Violetta from their chatter. They push me onto their stool, and one of them is trying to lift Luca's shirt off me. As I bat her hands away, she responds before I can tell her where to shove it.

"You can't wear that while trying these beautiful gowns on, darling." Cecilia tsks, clearly disapproving of what I'm wearing to start with.

The other lady, Violetta, is holding out a dress for me. Both turn to me, waiting expectantly. Reluctantly, I concede, and I immediately miss Luca's scent. I'm tired and don't have the heart to argue with these ladies who are just doing their job.

"Well, don't be shy," they say in unison. They stand beside each other, and I realize they must be twins. There are a few slight differences, but they're very much identical. Faking my confidence, I remove Luca's shirt, standing in my panties. Then they're pulling a dress over my head, while one is clipping and the other one comes to stand in front of me.

Gradually, I lift my head, seeing myself in the full-length mirror. It's shocking how much I look like a bride. I never thought much about my wedding day, so I have nothing to be disappointed about. But, the lack of my mother's presence pecks at my heart, making it the one thing I can be sad about. Thinking of my mother, guilt swarms me like bees in a hive. I've done everything she never wanted—accepted my father's money, and now entering into his world. All of her hard work over the years accounted for nothing in the end. I'm still where she never wanted me to be.

For as much as my mom refused to be in any man's control, I seem to have done the opposite of her. My life now depends on the enemy, on Luca. And I'm worried once this wedding goes through, I will become the enemy of the family I always resented but now wish I still had.

The sicker my mother became, the more my father stepped up in small ways. Ways that I greatly appreciated. Maybe if I wasn't so self-absorbed, I would have seen this happening right under my nose.

I shake my head, and the women take it as me saying no. The dress is pulled over my head, and another one is returned in its place. I begin to realize that I will never be able to get away from my family roots. I'll always be a mob daughter. I'll always be in some kind of danger. If I'm going to survive this, I need to be smart and kill before being killed.

I shake my head, and another one replaces it. The women coo at this one. Turning toward the mirror, my breath catches. I am stunning. This dress fits me like a glove already, no alterations required.

"This is the one," I whisper.

The women behind me clasp their hands together, smiling at me like I'm family. It's such a warm, kindhearted gesture that I tear up. These two ladies have shown me more kindness than most.

"You are going to make a lot of women jealous on your wedding day."

I think they're talking about my dress, but part of me believes they're also referring to Luca officially being off the market.

All three of us are staring into the mirror when the door opens with such force it hits the wall behind it. Luca storms in, shouting, "Out!" making all of us jump. The whole moment is ruined, and I'm brought back to reality.

The women scurry out and shut the door silently, leaving a stewing Luca in front of me. His hair is out of place, like he's been running his fingers through it. His features are sharp, his eyes a duller blue than before. I'm starting to learn that his eye color is his tell for the emotions running through him.

He's changed and is wearing a suit. I've never seen him dressed up like this. He's handsome on a normal day, but in this, he's sexier than hell. He shaved since I saw him last.

I swear he growls at me, and I take a step back. "What are you doing?" he demands.

I'm confused, not knowing if he's mad because I'm trying on dresses just like he requested. "Trying on wedding dresses?" I'm starting to think he's gone crazy. He's stalking toward me like a wolf. My whole throat contracts when I swallow, my heart beating heavily in my chest.

"Take it off!" he yells. I jump at the volume as fear starts to prickle my skin. I'm in way over my head. I'm not used to this life. I have a fleeting wish that I was brought up amongst the Mancinis. I'm underprepared for this new territory. I'm usually overprepared for everything. It's why I used to study so much. It's the reason why I aced every test ever placed in front of me. I stand with a tremble to my body, as I fear I will lose the one test that means the most in my life.

I watch as he bends down, pulling a knife out from under his pant leg. My feet stumble like they always do when I'm nervous. My lower half hits the bed before he's towering over me. I watch in horror as the knife is raised. Squeezing my eyes shut tight, I think of my mother. I pray for the family I never had that includes my father and Jonny. I even put his younger brothers in for the mental snapshot of how my life could have gone.

Instead of the cold dagger ripping into my heart, I feel my dress being pulled back from my pebbled skin. The smooth metal slides between my breasts before being yanking up once again into the fabric. My torso is pulled with each yank, and it takes all this time for me to realize the knife was never meant for my heart. My hands hold onto his broad shoulders, trying to steady myself. His face is set with determination with each sweep of his sharp knife that cuts the dress away from me.

The cold air that sprawls across my chest gives me the kickstart I need. I've never been one to back down. I'm silent when it works in my favor, but I've never been truly weak.

"What the hell are you doing?" I try to push him off me and succeed when he pulls the dress away from me completely, leaving me in my panties.

His hand wraps around my throat as my breath heaves. We're standing toe-to-toe.

A smile quirks the side of his lips. One brow lifts as he admires my body. I suck in a breath, watching his eyes fill with lust. I become painfully aware of the erection poking into me from his slacks.

His other hand's fingers drag down the side of my face like a feather. It's gentle, almost soothing, much like a lover might caress. I have to remind myself that these are the hands of a born killer. I can see it in his eyes that he wouldn't think twice about snapping my neck. But then his facial features soften, making him appear younger than normal.

His fingers trail down to my chest and circle around my pink nipple. Even without him touching it, they both become strained and taut.

I'm wet with arousal, and it confuses me. This man I hate, he is the enemy. Even though his hold is on my neck, he doesn't squeeze tight enough to hurt me. His motions are rough yet patient and smooth. It makes me feel warm and protected. I must be seriously messed up in the head if I'm feeling attracted to this type of behavior. Everything about this is wrong and makes me feel like a traitor. Traitors get killed. Everyone lives by that code.

His hand cups my breast, and I have to stop myself from leaning into his touch. His jaw relaxes, and a genuine smile is placed on display. It makes his suave, panty-dropping expression lethal. I have no doubt he's used to getting anything he wants with this face. It's hard not to melt to his every command.

"I'm going to make you feel really good. This is just a teaser of what our wedding night is going to be."

"I will never fuck you," I sneer just as he plunges two fingers into me. My panties a useless barrier. They're easily moved to the side.

"Your body says otherwise." I fight closing my eyes as his fingers stroke my inner walls with precision. "You see, everyone might see this innocent little nerd. But I see an empowered, sexy woman who can manipulate our world to fit her needs."

His words clutch on to my heart. When I bring my eyes up to him, a gateway opens, and I allow him to see deep into my soul. I watch as he crouches down, and his fingers part me. I've never had anyone go down on me like this before. His hot breath washes over my clit, as natural as if we've been lovers for years, and my fingers glide into his hair, his thick strands sliding between my fingertips.

His tongue licks me lazily, and a moan leaves me; my eyes close, enjoying this sensation. Long forgotten are my judgments of being a traitor, and they're replaced with a thirst for Luca's touch.

His tongue swirls my clit before he goes deep inside me, and his thumb puts pressure on my sensitive nub. I can't help but rock into him, needing the sensations he is bringing me. My legs shake while my body climbs toward climaxing. Just when I think I need more, his mouth latches on to my clit, sucking on it harshly as his fingers fill me. The two sensations rocket me over the edge as I fuck his mouth, and I scream out, "Oh my God!"

I'm delirious. His every touch is beyond good. My mind instantly goes to wanting his cock. Wanting to experience what it can do for me. I've heard the girls who work for me giggle about the guys they escort. The talented ones have them fighting for who gets the call.

"My name is Luca, not God," he says, wiping his mouth with the back of his hand. I'm thrown back into the present and realize I willingly allowed him to eat my pussy. Something no other man has ever done before.

"You ruined my wedding dress," I stand up for myself.

"You will be wearing whatever I tell you to."

I curse under my breath, and he grabs hold of my chin with his thumb and forefinger. "Such ugly words shouldn't come out of such a pretty mouth."

He then storms out of the room the same way he came in, ten times angrier than before, leaving me confused.

CHAPTER 14

LUCA

BURSTING OUT OF MY bedroom, I try to grasp some composure for myself. My thumb brushes across my lower lip, marveling at the knowledge that her pussy was on my face. My tongue darts out, tasting her lingering flavor on my lips.

Going down the stairs toward the now vacant kitchen, I confront the women I sent to help her. "You are not to be her friend. You are not to talk to her unless you have to!" I yell at them.

They keep nodding, saying, "Yes, boss." They dare not move, frightened of my outburst. No one understands. She is much more dangerous than anyone gives her credit for. I lost my head, seeing her in that dress, losing all control. Now, I imagine one of my men losing control. It could happen so easily. For that reason, I will have to order all the men to stay out of the house.

The talk about killing her, marrying her, having an heir is stuck in my head. It stews and festers like a tornado that refuses to dissipate. I had to see her. What I wasn't expecting was how goddamn beautiful she would be. She held the whole room's attention without any effort. The way her eyes lit up with fear and then hardened, trying to be my equal, snaked around me, adding to my fury. I held her thin throat in my hand, watching her eyes widen. She was scared, but I saw trust. A trust I don't deserve. I'm the last person she should trust. I saw the moment her fear changed into something else, and it was my undoing.

I have to stifle a groan at the memory of how her body responded to me, proving my theory of her infatuation with me.

Immediately, I order all the men out of the house. I walk through it on a mission, exercising the control I have in the family. They can stay outside until I say otherwise. My father says nothing, agreeing with my decision. It should have been this way with my sisters, but everyone is aware of the immediate death sentence if you look at one of them.

I refuse to go back to Aly. I won't give her that power. I need to leave some distance, prove to myself that she is a pawn in my game. She is here for a purpose, and I can't deviate from that.

S ITTING AROUND OUR LARGE dining room table, my father and I sit at each end. My mother is to the right of my father, with their oldest daughter, Aria. The three younger ones are on the other side. There are two years between all of us, and I'm the oldest.

"Why is our house so quiet?" my youngest sister, Gia, asks. She gives me that "I'm stirring the pot" smile of hers. She's eighteen and spoiled. My other sister, Katrina, who's twenty, giggles before I silence them with a glare.

I'm not good at taking jokes. Being a large Italian family, I've never moved out. It's easier to stay here when I have my separate wing and need to be here all the time. One day, when my father steps down, I will inherit this compound anyway.

"She might as well eat with us. This family can't keep a secret," Aria says. I realize Aly's age is right in the middle of my sisters. I bet they would get along under different circumstances.

"I thought you were marrying her, not keeping her prisoner?" Gia asks, being braver now that this is a family conversation.

"It's Luca's decision on what he wishes to do with the girl," my mother says. It may seem like she's allowing me to make the decision, but her tone says otherwise. She doesn't believe Aly should be kept prisoner. It's like she forgets she is still the enemy until we marry. I have nothing to tie her to me or our family until our vows.

The reason we haven't been bombed by the Mancinis is because they fear they might be bombing a place she is being held. There will be some sort of retaliation, and we need to be ready for them.

"She'll join us when I can trust her."

I swear I hear my sisters humming the childish song about a baby in a baby carriage, irritating me further.

"That's enough work talk for now," my father announces as he begins to dig into his meal.

The conversation turns, focusing on what my sisters are up to.

CHAPTER 15

ALY

SEARCHING THE ROOM I'VE been caged in, I confirm to myself that it's Luca's. It has his clothes, the sheets smell like him, and the bathroom holds products with similar scents. I've had time to inspect every corner, trying to find signs of who Luca Rossi really is. I don't mean the person he portrays himself as, but the one he hides. Everyone has a side they try to mask, and I want to learn his. It's the key to him and the real reason why I'm here.

When I find nothing, I stare at the door, anticipating him walking through at any moment. I stay up until my eyes can no longer hold themselves open, wanting to give him a piece of my mind. He never comes. I see no one. Food is brought to the room by one of the twins from earlier, but this time, she keeps her head down and mouth shut. Even when I try to talk to her.

It's been three days, and I'm starting to lose my mind. Like a dog who has been trained, I stand by the door, knowing the times they come. The door opens, and I smile at Violetta before checking past her to see if I can push my way out. She smiles at me, and I can instantly tell she read my mind. "He'll come around. When Luca doesn't understand something, it frustrates him."

I want to ask what she means, but the door closes, and that familiar click of the lock going back in its place comes.

Another day passes. I noticed some thread and a needle were forgotten, so I take up the job of sewing the dress back together. My mother sewed a lot of my clothing and taught me. I wonder if she's noticed I never came and saw her this week. I also wonder when my father's army will come in guns blazing to get me back.

My door clicks open, and I don't bother to see who it is. It's not until I hear the familiar Italian being spoken that I recognize it's the two ladies from before. Glancing over my shoulder, I see them rolling clothing in once again.

"He wants you ready in an hour," Cecilia says in English.

My dress is taken from my hands while my hair is pulled while being brushed.

"What are you doing?" I stand up.

"Why, we're getting you ready. It will be our jobs if you're not ready in time."

Grabbing the brush, I run it through my hair. I'm not used to this degree of so-called being pampered. Browsing through the clothes, I see they are all designer names. And I don't mean Gap, which in my world is as designer as I got growing up, much to my father's dismay.

These are thousands of dollars types of designer pieces. I run my hand over each one, trying not to smile. What can I say? I'm a girl who loves clothes.

Grabbing a pair of light-pink pants that are frayed along the thighs and a white shirt that falls off the shoulder, I put them on and feel more like myself. I wonder if he would let me go to my apartment. I need to get in contact with my girls.

I start to devise a plan. He's a businessman. If I talk to him, businesswoman to businessman, he's bound to understand. Once I check in with my girls and get my laptop, I can work from here until I figure out how to get away unscathed. I've been surrounded by powerful men like Luca most of my life. They don't give up without a fight. It's also why I'm the perfect madam. Everyone thinks I'm the geek who excels at numbers, who spends her time reading and allowing others to control her.

Well, I'm not that girl. I've been able to manipulate most men into thinking my ideas are theirs. I just have to allow Luca to believe he's won until I take it all away from him.

Going to the window, I open the blinds. Just like my father's men, some stay near the entrance, their guns on display. Farther out, there is a large metal gate with many men keeping watch.

Luca

I SIT IN MY father's office, along with him, our concierge, and my cousin Pauly. I'm having a hard time focusing, something that never happens. But all I can think about is how Aly's fingers raked across my skull and how her pussy clenched my tongue as I gave her a taste of what's to come.

"Send Mancini a wedding invite dated a month from now," I say, trying to push thoughts of Aly away for business.

"I thought it was next week," my dumbass cousin retorts.

"Follow it up with an engagement party two weeks from now. He'll make his play then." By then I will have Aly firmly on my side, and when I parade her around, she will fully be mine, her father no longer in her thoughts. She will choose me over him, and I'll get to watch it gut him. Then while he's weak, we can take over.

"Who are we inviting?" my father asks.

"All of the families," I reply, and my father seems to fight off a smile. For once, I think he may be proud.

He nods. "After the party, you will be made," he says, referring to me becoming a made man. That title alone makes me unstoppable. It gives me the license to do whatever the fuck I want. I'll be able to rise through the ranks and take my father's position when the time naturally comes.

"How do we know they'll even show?" Pauly questions with a half chuckle, as if he doesn't think they'll do as I predict. I have to refrain from pulling my gun on him. I have no idea how he's lived this long with his simple way of thinking.

"Mancini will use this as his opportunity to assassinate me and take his baby girl. The other families will simply want to watch and see who comes out on top. They'll want to find out which one of us is weak."

"We'll be ready for him," my father adds, backing me up. Standing up, I take the three steps toward him. Picking up his hand, I kiss it. My father is the smartest man I've ever met. He is the most respected as well.

My cousin follows on my heels, our shoes slapping against the tile floor until we reach outside.

"Hey, Smiley," he calls for my attention, using my nickname. Turning, I wait for him to continue. "I got a date this weekend, but she won't come unless her friend comes. How about you relax for once and get some tension off those shoulders."

Stepping into him, I say, "Are you fucking crazy? I'm about to be married, and you're asking if I want to go out on a date?" My hands curl into the jacket of his suit.

"I just thought you might want a night out. Didn't realize you liked the enemy's pussy."

My instinct is to pick up my gun. One hand uncurls from his jacket, moving to tighten around my gun, and I lift it to hold to his head.

"I'm your cousin, Smiley. We're family," he tries to remind me. Coward.

Never beg for your life. It shows weakness and makes me want to kill you more.

Instead, with my left hand, I punch him in the nose. I can hear the crack accompanied by the pressure hitting my knuckles.

"Don't disrespect my woman. Next time, I'll kill you, family or not."

He falls to the ground holding his face as blood gushes out. For good measure, I give him a kick to the stomach. "Be a man and clean up the blood without crying."

Tilting my head up, I see her beautiful face. She doesn't hide behind the curtains as I glare up at her. Instead, our eyes stay glued to each other's. The windows are soundproof, making it impossible for her to have heard anything I said.

My driver along with three bodyguards hop into my car along with me. I have a bigger target than normal on me now.

"Where are we headed?" I'm asked once I sit in the passenger seat.

"I need to buy some flowers." If my answer shocks them, they show no sign. "Hey, Vinny." I ask one of my bodyguards in the back, "What type of flowers does your wife like?"

"She likes the ones that come from me," he says cockily, busting my balls. Vinny and I grew up together. He's not Italian, but he's as close to me as my own family.

"Is this the part when you tell me to stay away from her?" I turn toward the back seat, showing him my smirk.

"If I had to, she wouldn't be mine." Truer words have never been said. "Sunflowers are her favorite. She hates roses," he answers my question. My initial instinct was roses. They're a classic but as uncreative as my dating life. That's the problem—I don't date. I don't buy flowers. I have no idea how to do this.

"Forget it. Turn around," I say to my driver, changing my mind.

"You scared of a little flower?" Vinny questions. My other two bodyguards are silent. If anyone other than Vinny questioned me, they'd have their nose broken like Pauly. But I respect his opinion. He's as close to a concierge as I have. He would have made it up higher in the family if he had the right type of blood flowing in his veins. The family's loss is my gain.

The driver begins to turn.

"What the hell are you doing?" I holler.

Vinny holds in his snicker, and we remain silent for the rest of the drive to the florist. I make my men hold the sunflowers, scared I might catch some feelings. I will be the ruin of Aly eventually.

CHAPTER 16

LUCA

O PENING THE DOOR, I find Aly sitting on the bed.

"You're late," she states, already like an old lady.

"I'm never late," I counter. She stands, and I hate everything she's wearing. She's hot as hell, but I prefer her in a tight pencil skirt and glasses. I like the nerd thing she normally has going on.

"Do you have contacts in?" I question, closing the door behind me. I'm about to fire the person who messed up my instructions.

"No," she answers, confused.

"Where are your glasses?" I swear I had a pair brought in here.

She has the nerve to roll her eyes at me. "I wear fake glasses. It's all part of my image," she says proudly.

I scoff. "Your madam days are over. I will not have a wife who is an escort."

"I'm not an escort."

I watch as her spine goes straight, and I swear her nails turn into tiny claws. My flowers hit my leg, reminding me I'm still holding them. Pushing them into her chest, I announce, "These are for you. Don't make me regret it."

"How romantic. Maybe you should have started with these, then kept your mouth closed. Practice what you preach, right?"

In one step, I'm crowding her space. No one disrespects me. She doesn't cower like my cousin. No, she sticks her chin out in defiance. I wrap an arm around her waist, bringing her in. Her heart pounds against my chest. She's frightened. Good. She's trying to even her breathing by stopping altogether. I can see the fear and courage fighting in her eyes.

"Disrespect me again, and I will bend you over my knee. I'll spank you until your ass is red with my handprint, then I will fuck you into submission. Understood?" My cock becomes a steel rod just thinking about fucking that tight pussy of hers. For good measure, I shift my hips into her, wanting to see how she reacts to me. Leaning close to her ear, I allow my lips to touch her lobe. "And when I fuck you, you'll be so wet for me I'll just slide right in. You may pretend you're this meek, innocent girl, but I see you. You like the challenge, and you like it when I talk to you like this."

The sound of her swallowing echoes between us.

Testing how far she'll let me go, I cup her sex. "If I dipped my finger in here, would I find you already wet?" I kiss down her throat, enjoying the way it pulses against my lips. I unfasten her button, and I slip my hand into her panties. Just as I thought, she's already wet for me. Sinking in two fingers, I tease her. Her hips struggle not to rock with my rhythm. I watch the hostility leave her eyes, and she gives in to me. Instead of bringing her to climax, I remove my hand to taste her on my fingers. Her eyes go wide, watching my movements.

"You have a minute to put yourself together. I don't want my men to see you all flushed, looking like you want to get fucked."

I turn my back, afraid she'll see the real me. My heart is pounding as fast as hers. She's changing me, and I hate every second of it. It makes me weak. If I can't focus, I will miss things. Missing shit makes me a dead man.

A frustrated growl leaves her pink lips. I'm pretty sure she called me "asshole" under her breath. I'm still trying to get my heart to slow down. I'll let her get away with it this time, because I'm preoccupied. And this is how it starts. I'm losing myself.

I need my shooting range to calm my heart. My blood flows violently through my veins with no outlet.

I grab her hand from behind me and yank her out of the room. She has to take two steps for each of mine. She's running to keep up with my quick strides. I expect her to complain or ask where we're going, but she stays silent.

I'm teetering on a very dangerous edge, and I wonder if she realizes this. I don't even fully comprehend why. This is her fault. Leaving the house, my men match my pace. I shake them off, telling them I'm not leaving the compound. I keep walking to the very back of the property.

When we reach the outdoor shooting range, Vinny appears out of nowhere carrying my guns for me. He's the best at what he does. I pick up my favorite sniper rifle. Using the scope, I set my sight on my target. Like the funny man he is, there is a picture of a sunflower as the target's bullseye.

Aly observes us, her eyes shifting between Vinny and me. Recognition of what Vinny has done takes root, and she dares to start laughing. "I like you." She smiles at him, her beautiful eyes tearing up and beginning to leak because she's laughing so hard.

"Get the hell out of here," I shout at Vinny. He begins walking away, and I aim my gun, giving him a warning shot. It whizzes right past his ear but doesn't touch him. That gets his ass moving. He starts running, and I shoot again. This time, it grazes his arm, and I listen to her gasp. It's hardly a wound. Nothing a little Band-Aid won't fix. When I turn back to Aly, she's no longer laughing. She stands still in shock.

"Come on," I tell her, grabbing her hand to pull her along once again.

I bring her to the bottom of my favorite station. It's high up in the trees with a tiny wooden platform.

"You good with heights?" I question as I place the strap of the rifle on, so it hangs on my back.

"I doubt I have much of a choice."

"True," I agree as I begin to climb up the nailed-in wood blocks that act as steps.

Once we both reach the top, we take a seat in the now crowded enclosure. Her arm pushes against mine in the tiny space I have. I'm used to having to shoot from small places people would never think of. She sits so her back rests against my legs, as her shoulders twist so she can look at me. I like that she doesn't try to hide herself. But in this small area, it's impossible.

Taking the gun from my back, I bring it to my front and offer it to her. She tilts her head cautiously before I can see her mind run wild. "I can pull out my other gun and press the trigger before you could pull yours. And that's assuming you don't miss." Pausing, I add, "I never miss."

"Then why hand me the gun at all?" It seems like a genuine question. I can understand where she's coming from. We've been born to think we're each other's enemy. Even with her not a part of her mob family, looks can be deceiving. She was always in the family. She just never realized it. She was still brought up with the same values I was. We just happen to be on opposite sides. But not for long.

"My wife needs to learn how to protect herself. Being able to shoot can determine whether you live or die."

She takes the gun off my hands, her fingers sweeping past mine. I expect them to tremble, but they're steady.

"I think you forget that I'm a madam and can already handle myself."

"You are not a madam," I grit out, hating that she even calls herself that. "And I protected you. You never had to learn to handle yourself."

"Honestly, I think you had a little too much creative power over this fantasy you have of us. You think you know me, but the truth of the matter is no one really does. Not you, not my father, no one. I don't even have a best friend. No one."

She brings up the rifle, resting it on the small wooden block I have set up for myself, and she fires the gun. Her body naturally absorbs the kick, and it's sexier than hell. Using my binoculars, I see she hit the target. Nowhere close to the bull's eye, but better than I anticipated.

"You're mistaken. I'm the closest thing you have to a best friend. And I saved your life by stealing you away."

Turning her head toward me, she arches her thin brow. I make sure to give her my arrogant grin before she goes back to concentrating on the gun. She reloads the rifle all by herself. I'm impressed.

"But is it really stealing when you have always been mine? Marrying Coy would have killed you inside. Do you honestly think he would let his wife be an escort?" I ask to keep annoying her. I realize I enjoy seeing how she reacts to my comments.

"For the last time, I'm not an escort. People respect me in my line of business."

"That's because they're hoping to get a piece of your ass. I'm the one who kept everyone in line for you. But now it's time you stop playing around and become my wife."

"I will never marry you. My father will kill you before it ever comes to that." She sounds confident in herself, her words grating on my patience. I have shown her too much mercy in the way she speaks to me.

"Oh, you will marry me. If you're not careful, it will be your father who is killed, not me."

The sassy smile disappears from her face. About time she takes me seriously.

I take the rifle from her and don't bother taking my time to line it up with the target. I've practiced so many times I could hit the bull's eye in my sleep. Staring at her, so she realizes what a perfect shot I am, I pull the trigger. I hand the binoculars to her and smile, watching her mouth drop open when she sees I hit it dead center. I never miss.

"I should have let my father deal with you when we first met," she says on a sigh, like that would have stopped how her future played out.

"But then you would have missed out on the love of your life." I shrug, watching her roll her eyes while scoffing. "Why didn't you ever rat me out?" I have often wondered. I would have been a dead man. I was too inexperienced back then.

"It was your eyes," she says after a short moment of silence. She has my attention. She shouldn't, but I'm more than curious right now. "I saw warmth in them. And I knew immediately you would never hurt me. So, I guess I decided to do what the old saying said. Keep your friends close but your enemies closer. I must have succeeded, since you think you're my best friend."

"Tell me then, who is your best friend?"

"I never had time for one of those. Most women wouldn't let their children play with me. They felt like they were choosing my mother over the Don, and that was too big of a risk. You see, it was my mother who chose not to accept his money, not the other way around. People didn't see that, and he allowed that to be her punishment." She's deep in thought, her forehead furrowed. Moving her hands in front of her as if getting rid of the bad air, she places a fake smile on her face.

"Don't do that," I tell her softly.

"Do what?"

"Pretend with me. I will always know when you're lying, even by omission. So don't pretend to be happy on my account. I can see that it hurt you."

"I suppose it does sting a bit. I honestly try not to think about it. I sound greedy even to my own ears. I was given every opportunity. I never lacked anything, and I felt loved by my mother. I've seen that some people have it harder than me."

I stare down at her lips, and I want to sample them so badly. She has this draw that I've never been able to escape. But I can't let her see the power she has over me. It will ruin everything I have worked for.

I place the gun back in her hands. "Try again," I demand forcefully, severing the invisible truce we had.

Chapter 17

Aly

FOR A SECOND, I thought we had a moment. I saw a glimpse of the old Luca who I originally met. But I was a young girl who was fascinated with the thought of having a crush on the enemy next door. I looked forward to the nights he snuck into my house. He was one of the rare people to treat me like I existed. He took time to check in on me, and each time he did, he placed himself in danger. Now, to think back on this, it all seems silly. I'm able to recognize others who did similar things, but I never gave them the credit.

Holding the gun up, I take my aim once again. His blue eyes never leave me, and his unique scent surrounding us causes my attention to be divided. His chest is against my back before his arms wrap around me, repositioning the gun. One hand covers mine, both our fingers hovering over the trigger.

"You need to steady your breathing." His voice is a low rumble. I try to by holding my breath then letting it out slowly. All of a sudden, I sound like the noisiest breather on the planet. It's all I can hear with him this close to me. "Don't stop breathing." His hot breath washes over my neck. "You need to learn to control your feelings, push everything away so the only thing in your vision and mind is that target."

Focusing on my breathing, I try to ignore that he's enveloped me with his entire body. It's like I'm wrapped in a blanket of Luca. The gun stops its slight vibration as I do as instructed. My finger presses down on the trigger as his hand slides up my torso. It throws off my focus. I don't even hear the shot hitting the target.

"Do it again." His voice is strong and determined. There's no point in arguing it's his fault.

Lining up the gun, I watch him out the corner of my eye. He's every bit as intense as he watches me. He never seems happy but always has a slight grin. It makes it hard to gauge what he's thinking or feeling.

Slowly, I'm able to block everything out. The trees, Luca, my thoughts. This will be my best shot of the day. Just as I'm about to pull the trigger, Luca's strong voice echoes around our quiet area. My fingers jump, pulling the trigger at the same time he announces, "We'll be married in five days."

I try to steady my heart and breathing to show no reaction. I knew he wanted this, the whole reason he kidnapped me, but it felt different. I almost laugh at my stupidity. Once again, I went into my fantasy world. I guess I forgot he was the enemy, even with me reminding myself. It went upon deaf ears and skipped past my heart. Marrying Luca will make me the enemy of my family. I'll never be able to see them again.

"Why are they important to you now yet never have been before?" he questions—they being my father's family, including Jonny, who is now dead.

When I dig deeper, it comes down to them being my family, and I felt bound to them.

"I'm the one who protected you and visited you the best I could from afar. They pushed you away every step, and I was the one always watching you."

My brain hurts, and I'm confused. He sounds like he wants this, like this isn't some ploy to get at my family. But if that were true, I wouldn't be a prisoner. They would have asked for a marriage pact.

"You don't know love." I refuse to meet his eye.

"Neither do you, little bird."

I'd like to think I do know love, but I realize I'm damaged. I'm the girl who would rather set up couples for money, all while never dating. I'm the girl who likes going over numbers and hiding in the shadows to use the information I find to my benefit.

I like taking risks, because I like the idea of being caught. Maybe that's why I never ratted out Luca when he was by the old oil refinery. The thought of my father finding out excited me, and the hope that Luca might return thrilled me in an unhealthy way.

"Come on." Luca is already climbing down the tree.

I hate that he's gotten inside my head. Stewing to myself, I follow after him.

He takes hold of my hand once my feet are on the ground, and we walk in silence to the house.

"Must you lock me in your room?" I ask. "You seem to have an army to keep me inside."

"It's not to keep you a prisoner but to keep you safe. I have some work still to do, but I will be coming to bed tonight." He catches me off guard. I had assumed I was staying in his room, but he hasn't been in there much since I arrived. "We might as well get used to sleeping in the same bed, as we will be doing that for the rest of our lives."

"Then what? You'll keep me in your ivory tower?" Silence meets my question.

"Have you ever been taken out on a date?" he eventually asks, changing the subject. I'm not sure where he's going with this.

"No." I allow my answer to hang in the air. I feel like this could be a trick question.

"We'll have our first official date tomorrow," he informs me, his tone making it sound final. We come to my door, and I don't want to be stuck in there all by myself. I'm tired of being left alone with my thoughts. I miss work. I miss using my brain.

Excitement begins to creep its way into me. I've never been on a date. I wonder if Luca will be the gentleman or the villain.

Either way, I finally get to be outside these walls. I could use the freedom to my advantage.

I WAKE IN THE middle of the night, and I can't move. It's like a heavy weight is holding me down on the plush mattress. I don't remember falling asleep, and it takes me a minute to realize that Luca has me caged in. One thick leg is draped across me, along with his arm, and he's curled almost on top of me like he's worried I'll run away. I take the opportunity to study him. He looks much younger when he's relaxed.

It's scary how much he hasn't changed in the last five years. I'm able to wiggle one hand out and brush some of his hair from his closed eyes. The man who lies beside me, I could easily fall in love with. But the man who he wakes up to be is scary. He's shown me kindness, but I'm not blind to what he's capable of.

For a moment, I don't think of the consequences of falling in love with this man. I curl into him, holding him too. For one night, I allow myself to pretend I don't belong to the mafia. I pretend I'm a regular girl having a sleepover with her boyfriend. Luxuries I was never afforded.

Chapter 18

Luca

"HEY, PAULY, YOU STILL wanting someone to double date with you?" Immediately, his face brightens.

"Yeah—"

Interrupting, I continue, "Good. Aly and I will be there."

He wants to argue, but I pin him with a glare that states if he says anything, I'll put a bullet in his head.

I'm on edge for most of the day. I need to shoot someone. It calms my heart in a way that no one and thing has been able to before.

"Where are you heading?" I ask, hoping Pauly is going out to collect from our associates. He's too stupid to do the torturing though. He'd forget some steps and get caught.

"Down to old man Vito's strip club," he says, jumping into the car. I start walking toward it, and my men follow suit. When I go to open the car door, he asks, "You wanting to bruise up those hands of yours?" He's staring at me over the roof of the vehicle. My cousin is a talker; if I give in to this, he'll talk my whole damn ear off for the rest of the day. My glare silences him for a moment, but not enough to stay that way. "We could use a guy like you today."

Walking into the club, I see a stripper grinding against the pole with some men scattered in the front row. I follow Pauly in. He's been here enough times to memorize the layout. He goes past the bar toward the offices. He kicks in the door, and we walk in.

"Pauly." Vito is all smiles until he notices me past my cousin. "The money is due today. Why you bring Luca?" he whines.

"You have the money?" I question, and Vito begins to trip over his words as I continue, "If you do, there is no need to worry about why I'm here."

"I will. I mean, I have it; it's just not here." His eyes go wide and volley between me and Pauly. They plead with my cousin to show mercy, but he doesn't beg. "Wait. Can I trade information for a time extension?"

"Information on what?" What I want to do is hit someone or, better yet, shoot him. Maybe in the leg, something insignificant but gets the message across.

"Mancini wants his daughter back. Coy paid him a lot of money to marry her, and he needs Coy's connections."

"Coy is the son of one of his top men. He already has the connections."

"There is fighting among the ranks. There is a struggle between the top bosses. That's why the marriage. To try to keep them tied together, to prevent an uproar. When Jonny died, people stopped looking to Mancini for the future."

Interestingly, there is fighting in the family. In my opinion, that's bad leadership. I could use this to my advantage. "I'll give you twenty-four hours."

"Thank you. Your kindness won't be forgotten," Vito tells me. I turn around, allowing Pauly to do whatever it is he does. One of the girls tries to catch my attention. My dick doesn't even stir. But as soon as I start thinking about Aly and the way she fights with me, I grow hard instantly. That girl has a mouth on her. One I want to fuck, among everything else.

I go to wait in the car, disappointed in the turn of events. Hopefully, our next stop is more to my liking.

By the time I get home, I have blood on my hands. The metallic smell of bullets and guns clings to me. Instead of going to Aly, I take a shower in the guest bathroom, uncertain how she would react. I want tonight to be perfect. I'm in no mood to fight. I want to relax and enjoy her company.

By the time I'm standing in front of my bedroom door, I find myself oddly excited. The last time I felt this way was when I had my first Christmas with my new family. This time, I made sure she was given her favorite types of skirts. I've been thinking about her all day and can't wait to see how her legs look in one of them.

CHAPTER 19

LUCA

OPENING THE DOOR TO my room, I see Aly is standing watch out the window. Her long hair has a slight wave to it, and the skirt she wears makes her round ass look delicious. My chest does a strange sputter as I walk deeper into the room. I was expecting her to be waiting for me, or at least acknowledge my presence. When I clear my throat, she turns toward me.

She shoots me an evil glare, her red lips protruding farther than normal. This girl thrives on hating me. It gives her a place to put her frustrations. Folding my arms, my legs spread, I silently challenge her to come out with it.

"Smells like you washed the blood off your hands." Her voice is so sweet, but I can hear the underlying venom in her tone.

Lifting my brow, I think, This is what has her panties in a twist?

She turns, giving me her full attention. She has on a tight sweater that accentuates her breasts and shows off her flat stomach like a second skin. Her legs have a silky-smooth shine to them, highlighting the way they go on for days.

"I've decided to let you roam the house from now on. You can stop plotting my death with your weak glare face." My voice is rougher than normal. She is dressed exactly how I like. In my favorite outfit of hers. She closes the gap between us, and I bend down, placing a kiss on her cheek before pulling back with a smile.

"How sweet of you." Sarcasm drips from her tone.

"It's the least I can do for my blushing bride."

Her eyes darken, and what I wouldn't do to see this girl flush crimson before me. To be able to see the vulnerability that lies in being shy and nervous from being in my presence. I want to be able to reach the softer side of her.

"You look creepy when you smile."

"I always smile."

This has her trying to fight one of her own. But her smirk says it all. She's saying I look creepy all the time. I may think I want the softer side of Aly Mancini, but there is no doubt this sassy side of her is addicting, and I thrive off her.

"What bugs you more: the fact that you actually like me, or that you're bad at pretending you hate me?"

Ignoring her eye roll, I take her hand, guiding her out of the room and the house, ending our conversation. She's taking it all in, no doubt memorizing the layout.

My cousin is outside, waiting for us. He's all smiles, thinking this is the greatest day. I'm normally all work and no play. I have a hard time sitting around when I don't see a purpose behind it. I'm always thinking of how my actions can move me forward. If I'm talking to you, it's because there is a need for it, not necessarily because I want to or I like the company.

I open the door for Aly, nodding for her to get in. I slide in beside her, so close our legs are touching. I like to fuck with her. She doesn't squirm away, pleasing me. In fact, she places her hand on my leg. Her affection puts me on alert as I wait for her to say what she wants. Or maybe she thinks I'm soft with her, so she can manipulate me. I play along, curious anyway. My arm goes around her shoulders like this is our every day.

Pauly drives us to his girl's house, and she has a friend waiting on the side of the road. I watch my cousin's eyes go to the girls, then to me. He doesn't say anything but jumps out of the car as soon as he puts it in park. Aly and I are right in the middle of the back, leaving no room for anyone else.

Instead of watching my cousin, I turn my full attention to the woman beside me. "You're beautiful." My eyes sweep down her body once again. "I've always loved you in a skirt."

"That's because you're like most men," she taunts, her eyes wide, her mouth set as if daring me to argue with her.

I lean into her, so she's the only one who can hear me. "Do most guys have you screaming out their name?" My fingers rest just above her cleavage. They lightly graze her skin for a moment. Her face flushes, pleasing me.

"You would know, since you stalked me."

My eyes narrow on her. "Admit it—you liked it."

She huffs out, frustrated with what I'm saying. My cousin's voice is heard through the closed windows. He's yelling at his girl, saying he told her he found her a new friend, so she didn't need to bring another one along.

The car doors open and slam shut. Pauly must have won, because no one tries to get in the back with us. He pushes down the gas pedal, and our bodies jostle. I hold onto Aly, making sure she stays safe.

"Where are we going?" Aly asks no one in particular.

"My brother-in-law is being honored tonight," the girl says excitedly from the front.

That's right. Her brother-in-law works high up in the bank and is as dirty as a greedy cop. But he has access to millions of dollars. A lot of people use him to clean their money. We do most of our laundering with our many companies. But sometimes we make too much and need to go another avenue. He is on our side and is always willing to help—for a fee, of course.

His vaults hold shit that can't always be documented. It's like the hidden cave filled with gold that no one ever knew about. Stolen gems, gold, and paintings sit in his trust until the day the cops stop sniffing around you, to allow you to sell it to the right buyer.

The thing is, the bank is in Mancini territory. It's an anomaly. The bank is like Switzerland, a neutral zone for all gangsters. No matter what, everyone is welcome. Although, not everyone uses the resource to their full advantage for whatever reason. I guess it comes down to trust.

Coming to the bank, the beautiful architecture is on full display under its white glowing lights. Stepping out, I give Aly my hand to help her. Vinny watches my back as he comes from the car behind us. I'm being cocky, showing up here with Aly. I can't help it. I want them to see her on my arm, and there is nothing anyone can do about it. My bodyguards are in the other car, waiting outside on alert. With events like these, no weapons are allowed. Not even I can get a gun through the metal detectors.

"No matter what, do not talk to anyone here," I tell Aly as we walk in. I want to see her reaction. She's beginning to trust me, and I want everyone to see it. I've been able to do what her father has been trying to for years, and I did it in just over a week.

"Why?"

"Because I said so." I pull her so our bodies are touching, resembling a lover's embrace. "Disobeying me can get you killed. We're walking into a roomful of men who wouldn't think twice about putting a bullet in someone else to further their gain." She visibly swallows, taking my warning seriously. "Good girl."

The wind blows her hair out of place, and I move it behind her ear. My fingers skim her neck as I gaze down at her. My other hand moves from the small of her back to holding her elbow. I watch the light pulse in her neck pick up its pace. I want to mark her, for everyone to understand she is now mine. I want to destroy her in every way she has destroyed me. I'm starting to realize I won't be able to go back to the old Luca after this, and it's all her fault. Behind my eyes, a throb is starting to be felt as my anger rises at the situation, at her, and at myself for being so stupid to allow her in. I begin to question my empathy and affection that has taken root deep inside of me. She's now like the etched tattoo you regret that's inked on you forever.

Moving out of her space, I take note of how hard my heart is beating. Possessiveness consumes me, and no one is around to set it off. We finish walking the rest of the way in silence, and I don't recognize I'm squeezing her too hard until she whispers, "My hand." Her poor fingers are white from my hold. Releasing my grasp, I try to refocus.

Scanning the crowd, I immediately spot Coy and his father at the back of the room. They haven't seen us yet. I don't think anyone expects us to be out in public.

I walk us to the makeshift bar, ordering her a glass of red wine, just how she likes. And I have a whiskey on the rocks.

The son of the Russian mafia sees us, and his eyes light up. Even among the elite of the underworld, the other important families keep loose enough track of each other to see I'm taunting the Mancinis.

"I hear congratulations will be in order soon." The Russian leers at Aly, and I hate it. I use all of my self-control to not knock him out. "It's a pity we weren't invited."

I shake his hand. "There are too many Italians who need to be there."

He laughs stiffly, giving off the vibe he believes he's been disrespected. He shouldn't, but this could be the tipping point if they perceive us Rossis as weak. They may try to overrun our family.

When he leaves our side, Coy is staring at us. He's bad at hiding his resentment. There is no doubt he was just patting for the gun he isn't wearing. Aly hasn't seen him yet, and I use this to my advantage. Tilting my head down, I give her a soft kiss on the lips.

She doesn't pull away, delighting me. She tastes like dry red wine and that unique taste that can only be described as her. My lips leave hers, and I enjoy the flush that begins to creep up her neck.

Leaning into her, I ask, "How is it that you blush when I kiss you, but you call yourself a madam?"

Taking a sip of my whiskey, I enjoy her glaring eyes on me, but she has a hint of a smile. Out the corner of my eye, Coy is starting to make his way toward us. Happy he saw the kiss, I lead Aly toward the balcony, where the light is dim.

Without being obvious, I check that no one is trailing Coy. He is falling perfectly into my trap. Aly walks to the ledge overlooking the city lights. Coming up behind her, I place my arms on the balcony beside her, caging her in with my body.

Chapter 20

Aly

HAVING LUCA'S ARMS AROUND me is a comfort I wasn't expecting. I was caught off guard by the overwhelming nervousness I felt as soon as we walked inside and I saw people I knew. His warmth is what's keeping me from shaking. Breathing in the city air, I try to focus on Luca, duplicating how he made me focus when teaching me to shoot. For once I feel like someone actually has my back for me and not the connection I have to my father. I have no doubt Luca would give his life for me. I must be losing my mind. Taking in another ragged breath, I push back into him, using his presence as a safety blanket.

Since Luca kidnapped me, I began to think about the static phone calls I'd been receiving and the notes that tried to spook me. I feel so disconnected from the world; I wish I knew if my girls were all right. I'm going to be losing clients soon with the radio silence I've been forced to give.

"Aly." The deep voice doesn't come from Luca. His body stiffens behind me. I try to turn, but Luca keeps me in place. Taking his time, he turns both our bodies, keeping me under his arm.

"Coy," Luca remarks, his voice sinister, and the smile he gives would be described as deadly.

Their attention is no longer on me but each other. Even with the warmer air, I shiver. Luca holds me tighter beside him. The tension is so heavy I have no doubt one insignificant spark will produce an explosion.

"You have what's mine," Coy growls. Mafia men dislike when something is taken from them. Coy is no different.

Luca tsks. "She is by my side, kissing my lips. I would say she's mine," Luca counters, sounding cheerful.

My heart begins to pound, panicked of the outcome. The overwhelming heat pouring through me with Luca's arm around my shoulders is causing me to sweat. My gut is telling me to move, to welcome the cooler air, but I know better. I take in the area. Luca's friend from the car stands on the outskirts of the balcony. The constant chatter of the room has lowered, and several eyes have been pulled toward our quiet altercation. There is a war waging in both Luca and Coy's eyes. Warnings flare vibrantly in my head. The sensations of crawling tingles prickle my skin. I'm forced to ignore the creepy, imaginary vibes of hundreds of spiders swarming my body, and I bite into my lower lip. I refuse to scratch the feeling off while staying in the safety of Luca's arms. Even here, I don't get the comfort I'm hoping for. His touch is too light, and his heat is too stifling.

Coy catches my eye. A mixture of anger, hurt, and betrayal shines through them, causing my stomach to drop. Immediately, I cast mine down to avoid it. Luca's fingers dig into my shoulder, sensing that I'm starting to fall apart. It's not that I feel anything toward Coy, but the guilt that I'm betraying my family hits me. It's a feeling worse than being a rat and thinking you're about to be caught. We've all been brought up with similar neighborhood values. Snitches get stitches.

I don't have a side I belong on now. Does this make me the enemy? I've always listened and done what I was told—for the most part. I thrived on being told I was doing a flawless job. All of this is overwhelming and confusing. I have no idea where my loyalties lie.

If this makes me the enemy, then maybe this makes Luca more important to me.

"Come home, Aly." Coy's deep, rich voice startles me while I'm ranting to myself inside my head.

Luca loosens his hold on me as if daring me to go. Both men are staring expectantly at me, waiting for me to make my choice. Luca takes a step away, making it clear that I'm deciding myself without his influence. I swallow, my saliva thick in my throat. I'm almost scared I'll choke on it. Luca's eyes are a deep blue, their depths holding me in place. My heart picks up its pace at the intensity of it all.

I'm watched in deadly silence. Luca is calm, almost unaffected, while Coy's jaw tics as he clenches. For all the years I have known Luca, he has never lied to me. He's always watched out for me. Something has me not moving. Rolling my bottom lip in, I nibble on it, recognizing either way I am fighting a losing battle. This has nothing to do with love but with showing who has power. The toxicity of the air rises with each second, and I remain frozen. Chancing another glance at Luca, I see his eyes are on Coy. Swallowing sharply once more, I refuse to go with my promised betrothed. I can't guarantee I would be safe.

Luca snickers, and I peek at Coy. He has this one vein in his neck that throbs when he's angry. His face has a slight redness to it. He's not happy. Coy takes a step toward me, and Luca steps in front of me. "She's made her decision. I suggest you leave my bride alone."

"This is far from over," I hear Coy say. "We will be seeing each other soon, Aly."

I don't realize I'm holding my breath until Luca turns to me. His hand cups my face. I don't know what he's searching for. He must be happy with what he sees, because he places his lips against mine. This kiss is hard and demanding, like he's trying to take my soul with his by the end of it.

"Let's go," he says as he pulls me into a hug. It comforts me once again like a safety blanket. My eyes fill with tears, and I hate that I'm showing weakness. I'm used to dealing with stress; this reaction is silly. I'm a strong woman. Yet, I'm exhausted from the altercation.

Holding my hand, he leads me through the crowd of people pretending to have conversations, when in fact their eyes are on us. I have this feeling of dread, like I'm being watched. Like this is more than a crowd of nosy gangsters. Checking over my shoulder, I see Coy is staring us down. Even when we step out, my body is aware I'm being watched. It's the same feeling I'd been having over the last month before there was any talk of weddings.

Luca's men are staggered outside and within our path as we head for the car. The same guy and girl are behind us, and I can hear the girl complaining that we just got here and she doesn't want to leave.

The front is vacant. I half expected my father to be there once we stepped out. Along with my exhale, three cars rush in front. Tires squeal, and I'm frozen in place. Gunshots are being fired, and a bunch of men seem to appear in the street like they were hiding.

Luca throws his body over mine like a protective shield. I hit my head on the steps. My vision doubles, and it makes me fuzzy on what's happening. My body is being pulled away from the open steps, my feet tripping over one another. Men rush around, scattering to where they're needed. Luca's smell clings to me, even though he's no longer holding me, but I can still feel him nearby.

"Get her out of here!" His deep voice is full of rage. Turning my head, I search for his voice as he comes back into view. He places a kiss on my lips before someone is pulling me away from him. It's a madhouse in the front. Everyone is shooting at everyone.

The guy from the car, who I wish I was introduced to, places me by some hedges. His girl is here too and is hysterical. I should be frightened of dying, but instead, I can't help but think of my home, my sanctuary. The man's back is to us as he shoots his gun. If I'm going to get away, this is my chance.

Taking in my surroundings, I'm aware the fog in my head is starting to dissipate, and I notice blood on my hands. Checking myself over, I don't feel pain. Touching the hysterical girl, I wipe some of the blood on her by accident.

"Have you been shot?" I ask, making her scream louder. The man turns from his spot, trying to get her to quiet down. This is my chance. While he's distracted, I sprint away.

I can hear him yelling at me and footsteps before gunfire erupts all around me. I'm shocked I haven't been hit. I run as fast as I can. My lungs burn, my legs pumping, and I keep going. I don't stop until my building comes into view. I must have run a mile. The only sound now comes from the hard floppy steps I take. My breath burns down my whole throat. I believe I heard that someone once died from running too hard.

I push the buttons on the wall, hoping someone will ring me in. I have no keys. Someone unlocks the door without checking. This is something I would normally complain about, but today, I'm relieved. Walking in, I see no one is around. I head to my private elevator. My feet want to slide out from under me from hurting so much. I punch in my key code, locking me inside my home, before I allow myself to slip down the wall. My feet pulse, each breath strained.

I sit there for a long time. It takes all my willpower to struggle and stand back up. I need water and to check my laptop. I need to be certain I still have a business. I should call my father, but something is holding me back.

CHAPTER 21

ALY

ONE OF THE REASONS I like living in an apartment is the noise from all sides surrounding me. That constant strum of movement helps lull my mind when it runs too wild. Tonight, the world is void of sound. I check my hearing by running the faucet for a glass of water. My fingers tap on my glass. How is it that I feel guilty, when everyone uses me for whatever purpose they need? Yet, this gnawing feeling stays with me.

My skin is peppered with goose bumps that refuse to leave. I swear the temperature is ten degrees colder than normal. Closing my eyes, I start going through my mental checklist of what I need in here.

"Well, well. You are a survivor after all."

My first instinct is relief; it seeps into my bones. But when I turn, there is hate in his eyes. Those hard, cold gray eyes wash the momentary relief away, leaving goose bumps on my skin.

Jonny isn't here to protect me.

I know this Jonny; I've seen this version before.

"I thought you were dead," I prompt, realizing I'm isolated and alone.

"And you planted yourself right in my shoes, ready to take my spot."

My eyes snap to his, finding him coming closer. His devilish lips are straight, his pale, narrow face unremorseful. I never realized Jonny hated me this much. I never caught on that he was driven to remove me, the so-called thorn in his side.

"That's not true." I set my glass down, fear starting to eclipse my soul.

"You are the dead weight of our family. Cozying up to Coy, so then he would marry you. I never thought you would have the balls to repeat your actions with the enemy. Then play with both sides to see what suits your needs better. You're the leech that sucks the good out of people. I've seen enough. This was a test, one you failed miserably. All while proving my father is no longer capable of ruling over the family anymore. He's too old and soft."

I look around to see something I can use for a weapon. When I bring my eyes back to my brother, I watch as they flicker with an evil type of happiness. One that thrives on hurting other people.

"This would have been so easy if you were shot on the steps, or if you stayed in the damn car." My stomach turns in a hauntingly painful twist as I realize he was trying to get me killed. "Everything would have played out how I wanted. Me, the son coming back from the dead, and you would have been forgotten, forever. In all honestly, they should have killed your mother as soon as she tried to trap my father."

"She did no such thing. She never wanted anything from him," I defend her without even thinking about it.

"And yet, she is what divided their relationship. He had to protect you. His only daughter. His precious gem."

My head is still foggy from hitting it on the ground. I knew Jonny never liked me, but I didn't think he wanted to kill me. My stomach pinches, realizing we've come to an impasse.

He watches me as I look for a weapon once more, as he brings out his gun. I have a knife in a block that is closer to him than to me. My brother narrows his eyes, flashing with smugness, but he doesn't smile. I watch him bring his gun out, goading me.

"Father loves you. He's groomed you to take over," I say cautiously, trying to make short movements he won't notice.

He nods, his voice eerily calm. Much calmer than my own. "True. I've become wiser than him. When he is killed, he will realize he let his guard down too much. You were the start of that."

"Why kill him?" He's sounding crazy. I keep moving slightly, trying to stay out of the path of his gun.

"He likes his power. He won't step down. He doesn't think he needs to. If he did, I could accept him."

"What about family values? Your mother?"

"She will understand. When he allowed a bastard child to live, he didn't choose those so-called family values. Why should I honor them if he doesn't?"

My door is kicked in with a booming sound. My heart soars, hoping for Luca, but it's one of my brother's men. I watch the intruder kick it back closed, but it doesn't latch from his original unnecessary force.

"Luca has been dealt with" is grunted out.

Jonny nods, raising his gun. "Should I shoot you now? Or should I bring you to Coy? He's crazier than me. No one has ever lived after two-timing him. Or should we stage it to seem like Luca killed you, then Coy killed him?"

Fear is firmly rooted in me. He sounds like he's speaking the truth.

"Do you want money?"

"I don't need your money, Aly. But I do appreciate all the work you did for it. I will be taking your business over. You have some nice young women working for you. I'll have to test each one out. See if they pass the quality check." He winks at me. "Hold her," he commands his man. I try to run past him, but he grabs me hard, pulling my hands behind my back.

My brother is being arrogant, and he's enjoying playing this out. I try to scream, but a large hand covers my mouth. I bite down on the flesh, tasting his blood. He curses and hits me upside my head. For the split second his hand leaves my face, I scream and yell, all while trying to kick him in the nuts.

"I never did teach you any real skills," Jonny says right in my face.

Jonny hits me there with the blunt end of his gun. My cheek swells with hotness and radiates pain, coursing down my body. It shoots up my arm as I'm pulled tighter.

I scream again, tears fresh in my eyes. Jonny raises his arm to hit me once again, and the door bursts open once more. I expect to see Coy wanting his revenge on me, but it's Luca. He's holding his side, with blood seeping through his clothes.

His eyes are full of rage I have never seen before. He charges Jonny, and my brother shoots. The shot misses, skimming Luca's arm. It must sting, but I don't see any blood—at least not yet.

My leg kicks up behind me, having the element of surprise, and my heel goes up hard. Luca shoots the man holding me point-blank. Blood splatters on me, and my body freezes. I tell myself to run, to do something, but I can't.

"Aly." Luca's voice has my eyes going to him and Jonny. They're fighting, and Jonny's gun falls to the floor. Luca hits him twice, square in the nose, and then Jonny pokes his fingers into his side. Luca cries out in pain, giving Jonny the upper hand. Now he has Luca pinned. Scrambling to get the gun, I hold it in my hands. Jonny is choking Luca, his face going from red to purple. Luca is trying to say something, but it comes out garbled with his throat being closed.

Raising the gun, I breathe and focus as Luca taught me. Jonny keeps squeezing, unafraid that I'm holding a loaded gun. Holding my breath, I pull the trigger with all my might.

CHAPTER 22

LUCA

I WATCH ALY BRING the gun up. She stands tall above the two of us, her hand mirroring the way we both scramble on the floor, hoping to get the upper hand. She never leaves my sight as I fight off Jonny. It gives him the advantage for now. Her arm is unsteady, her eyes unfocused, going back and forth between us. I watch her blow out her breath and do as I taught her. Her trembling slows but doesn't stop; she closes her eyes, making me say a quick prayer that she is still able to shoot under pressure. Her finger closes in on the trigger, testing the shot, but it takes three times before she pulls with enough force. Her forehead pinches the moment she decides, her eyes opening, and I squeeze mine shut, going limp under Jonny. With her trembling, I can't tell where the bullet will be flying.

When its sound booms in the room, I'm able to kick Jonny off before I'm able to realize it never hit me. Jonny reaches for his thigh, cursing at her. Taking my knife out, I hold it up to his throat. I hesitate, waiting for Aly to tell me no. The realization that I'm waiting on her makes me feel spineless, like I've lost my edge. I would have never given anyone that type of power over me before. When she doesn't say a word, I save both our lives by slitting his throat. I allow him to fall to the ground with a thud, and I step over him to grab my girl. I hold onto her arm, pulling her with me.

I usher her down the stairs, her tiny frame shaking. I have Vinny waiting for us. The leather seats are cold as I slide the two of us into the car before he rips out. The night is dim with a few streetlights around, the air pinching our skin with its crispness. My hand never leaves Aly, her frame shaking violently. I allow myself to stew, my internal emotions raging from all the errors tonight. We look sloppy, inexperienced, and incapable. My fingers coil into my palm and out, thinking how much Pauly's error will cost him. There was no reason for her to be lost and allowed to run away. I trusted my cousin with her life, which means more than mine at the moment. Frustrated that we had security outside and we were still blindsided, I run my hand through my hair. Shit like that can't happen.

If Mancini thinks his daughter is dead, he'll be storming our compound. Him believing that his two children are dead will cause him to react immediately and not hold anything back. Before tonight, I still felt like Aly would be safe with her family if something happened. But now, it's clear she is safest with me.

Jonny dead in her apartment is not good. I don't have time to call in a cleaning crew. Aly will be blamed for killing him, and blood will be spilled to avenge him.

I hold her tight, her body vibrating into mine.

"Where are we headed?" I ask Vinny. We're going in the opposite direction of the compound.

"The safe house. You need someone to take care of that open wound you have going on there. And I can't promise the compound is safe yet."

I use my free hand to push on my stomach. I'm drenched in blood. I hadn't had time to register that the blood on me was mine. I'm more lightheaded than I would like. Vinny pointing out my wound makes my body realize I'm hurt. The radiating, scorching burn begins to move outward, making its presence known to me. I keep my hand on it, trying to stop the bleeding, all while never dropping my hold on Aly. I'm not worried about myself; all that matters is her.

When we stop, Vinny tries to help, but I shoulder him away. "Help her," I grunt out. Any movement now hurts like a bitch. It feels like there is a fire in my stomach. I'm slow and need to grab hold of the railing to climb up the two stairs.

The door opens, and out walks the doctor. He reminds me of a skinny Santa Claus, with his white, long hair that matches his full beard. He's a hermit, and we allow him to stay in our safe house. He helps me inside, placing me in his examination chair. I close my eyes, nervous I might pass out from the blood loss.

The doctor turns on the light; it's blinding, forcing me to squeeze my eyes tighter. My shirt is being cut off my body. There is pressure on my side, and I want to scream out in pain, but I hold it in. I might have moaned, but I can't be too sure. With each cleaning swipe and each poke of the needle, the pain intensifies as I get stitched up. Time fades in and out as I focus on each feeling I have.

Aly

I'M PLACED IN A dim room with a cup of warm tea in my hand. I can see where Luca was taken, the bright light seeping into my area. He's in there for a long time. I start to get worried that he may not make it. I never did check to see how badly he was hurt. It concerns me that he doesn't make any sounds. I can hear the doctor and Vinny talking, but their voices are too muffled to hear what they are saying.

If Luca didn't find me, I would be dead right now. I owe him my life. My body still has a slight tremble to it, but for the most part, I'm able to control it a lot better.

My legs are curled up in the chair they sat me in, my eyes never leaving the door as I wait. I could run and leave, but I don't have the energy. If I'm being honest with myself, I also don't want to. I need to see if Luca is okay. He deserves that type of respect.

Eventually, I watch Vinny and the older man bring Luca out. He's half unconscious, his feet barely moving as they carry his weight across the room to the other doorway. I can hear the creak of the bedframe as they lay him down. I'm forgotten in the other room as if I don't exist. The two men come out, talking to each other in front of me, never sparing me a glance.

"I'm going to head out for the night," the doctor says. "I'll be back to check on him later."

The other man nods, shaking his hand. "I'll be staying to make sure we get no trouble here."

The two men walk out the door together, leaving me by myself.

Standing up, my legs are stiff from being tucked in. I walk to Luca. His eyes are closed, his breathing shallow. He's shirtless, and even relaxed, there is a valley of muscles along his torso. Taking off my now dried bloody clothes, I slip into bed with Luca. I curl up to him, his heat radiating back to me. Carefully, afraid I might hurt him, I place my head on his chest, listening to the steady rhythm of his heart. It lulls me to sleep.

Chapter 23

Luca

W HEN I WAKE UP, my body is sore as hell, and I'm hot. I've kicked off my covers, yet the heat stays in my core. Trying to shift my body without too much movement, I begin to feel light breaths on my chest. Turning my head, Aly has curled herself into me.

I lie there enjoying her beside me, allowing my smile to be apparent on my face. My hand comes up and holds her, my fingers touching her soft skin on mine. She's wearing a bra and I'm assuming panties, but the rest of her body is naked, touching mine.

I'm just in my boxers, and my cock hardens further, having her cling to me. I can't take my eyes off her. She is painfully beautiful. Her dark hair fans down her slender neck, her pouty lips soft and pink. Her lashes are thick and fall across her skin, showing her youth and innocence. My heart thuds faster, my mouth dry from seeing her.

Since I laid eyes on her, I've been drawn in, needing to learn everything about her. I couldn't help myself. Each time I would come to see her, I knew I shouldn't be there, yet it happened time and time again. Having her in my presence calmed me in an eerie way. I like it way more than I should.

I expected her to be scared, to send me away, but each time, she stood her ground, challenging me in a way no one had before. Deep down, I knew she was trouble for me. I knew I would never let her go. I've often wondered how my path would be different if she didn't take that shortcut all those years ago.

As she begins to move, my hands rub up and down her smooth, warm skin. I love the way it feels under my calloused hand. The contrast is strikingly addicting under my palm. We're still pressed tight together, my erection poking into her upper thigh that's draped across me.

I wait to see her next move, if she'll pull away from me. Instead, she lifts her face to me.

"Good morning." My voice is gruff from just waking up.

A small smile widens her lips. My eyes are drawn to them, and I get this drive to claim her as mine. I'm forced to remember she was almost ripped away from me. I grip her face on both sides, and she willingly comes up to meet my lips. I kiss her as if I own her. My tongue licks her lips before I forcefully invade her mouth. I wait to see if she'll bite me in any way. Her body melts into me, her weight shifting over me, so I'm forced to look up at her. My hands roam her back, cupping the soft flesh on her ass before making my way up top to tangle in her hair.

She doesn't put up resistance as I was expecting. She seems to be fully accepting that she is mine. It does something strange to my heart. My hand cups the back of her neck, pulling her down to me. I kiss her harder, her apex just above my hard cock. It keeps bumping into her. My stitches below my ribs tighten as I begin to move.

I pull down the cup of her bra, and my mouth closes around her delicate, delicious nipple. I ignore the straining of my wound as I slightly sit up. I suck harder, feeling the pucker of her skin, and love the way she wiggles above me from my touch. My tongue flicks it as my hand unclasps her bra.

She's so soft against me. Grunting, I flip her under me, taking control. One of my stitches stretches through the skin, but I don't care. I pull her panties to the side, slipping in two fingers. It makes me crazy to even think someone has touched what's mine before I even had the chance.

Her pussy is smooth, perfectly groomed. She's so tight, her velvety walls warm. I've never felt anything like her before. Her breathing slows as my fingers leisurely move in and out of her. When my digits are nice and wet, I rub them against her clit, making her groan in pleasure. Aly is so responsive to me, always has been, even when I didn't touch her.

I knock her legs farther apart with mine. Sitting back, I get a nice view of her perfect virgin pussy. She smells intoxicating. It was for this moment I beat the shit out of the first man who tried to steal what was mine. I watch as my fingers thrust in and out, her breathing accelerating.

Dipping down, I taste her. She is the most exotic thing I've ever eaten. It's addicting. Her head tilts backward at an uncomfortable angle as her back arches with each stroke of my tongue.

Sliding off the bed, I drop my boxers, loving how her face lights up seeing me naked. She's flushed, looking gorgeous. Going back, I rip off her panties, wanting her whole body bare to me. Her chest rises and falls, her perky breasts bouncing.

I begin to feast on her again, her body doing short, calculated thrusts into my face. Her whole body trembles, her legs kicking out, trying to get extra friction. My tongue flicks her sensitive nub as my fingers thrust into her. She cries out my name, her fingers tugging at my hair with sharp tingles scraping my scalp.

My dick is raging hard, twitching in my palm as I tug at it. Aly's big gray eyes stare up at me with adoration and lust. I've never seen this expression on her before. Climbing up onto her, I rest my thick head at her entrance. I move it up and down, coating it with her wetness. She is staring at me intently, waiting for me to claim her. I push in, trying to be slow and gentle, but my brain doesn't seem to be working for me. She cries out, and I still once I've fully entered her.

I kiss her lightly before licking the lone tear that escaped the corner of her eye. "Are you okay?"

She nods, moving her body under me. Her walls clamp tightly around me, making it almost impossible to move without coming. I kiss her everywhere. Not leaving any skin untouched as I thrust into her. I've never looked into a woman's eyes or face as I fucked them before. The intimacy is unnerving, like I'm giving her whatever good I might still have in me to her. I'm willing to take any part of her soul that could be damaged in return, but I doubt there is any.

Her body trembles in my arms while her pussy clamps down on me hard. My balls draw up, and that tingling at the back of my spine tells me I have no choice. I can feel my hot cum exploding into her at the same time she calls out my name. She's loud and unreserved, and I hope everyone can hear her. Then they will recognize she is mine. As soon as she takes my name, the world will realize they can never fuck with her again.

I would kill even my own family if they crossed her.

Falling back to the mattress, I gain my breath. We're both sweaty. And it's in this moment there is no question that I love Aly. I never thought such a thing was possible. But concluding that I would kill anyone for her shows me how much I am invested.

"Did I hurt you?" I ask.

"Not as much as I expected," she says shyly. I don't think I have ever seen her be shy. My hand goes to my side, and I realize I'm going to have to be stitched up once again.

Aly

MY HEART IS PALPITATING as Luca and I lie next to each other. I never knew you could show so much emotion through your body. I figured one day that Luca and I would have sex. But I always imagined it as hate sex. Not what we just did. It felt an awful lot like making love. Sitting up, my legs and the rest of my body are sore. Looking over at him, I notice he's bleeding again. My hand lightly circles the area, wishing I could take away all of his pain.

"I'm fine," he murmurs, moving my fingers away.

I shift to put my legs over the bed, needing to go to the bathroom to clean up. When I stand, I notice a smear of red blood on his sheets. Light pink also marks my thighs from Luca being my first.

"Stay in bed. I got this," he says with a grunt as he stands. He's back to staring at me with rough determination that has me lying back down. There is no room to argue with him. I can't help but smile, enjoying the way he tries to be a gentleman. He's rough around the edges, but it makes it sweeter.

He comes back with a washcloth and cleans me up. I have never seen Luca take his time or act as if I'm made of glass before. It's endearing.

Just as he finishes, the door swings open, causing me to scream. I try to cover myself up as fast as I can. Luca hollers, sounding like an angry bear before he's punching someone in the face.

He's still buck naked and slams the door behind him, pulling whoever that was out. I don't move, waiting to hear a shot, but nothing comes. No one seems to be yelling back at him. Slowly, my heart rate starts to come down. I quickly put on my clothes before sitting back on the bed. I wait there for what seems like an hour until Luca comes back, wearing a new pair of shorts. His knuckles are red, and his stitches need to be redone.

CHAPTER 24

LUCA

W E STAY AT THE safe house for three days. It's become our private bubble where Aly and I exist with no one else. My side isn't as sore, but I still have to be careful with the stitches. When it's time to leave, we drive to my family's compound and walk through the door, holding hands. As insignificant as that may seem to anyone else, it's a big deal.

I'm no longer saying she's my prisoner but mine to possess. I watch my sisters trying to hide their smirks. They need to get out and have a life of their own if my love life is their entertainment.

My whole family welcomes her, kissing her on the cheek. When my father reaches out and gives her a hug, my whole body relaxes. If I'm being honest, it's only my father's opinion that matters. He's the don of the family. All of our lives are up to him.

"Aly, so nice to meet you," he tells her. "I look forward to your wedding tomorrow."

She stills for the briefest of seconds. But enough that I notice. She may have forgotten about that, but I haven't.

"Aria, you and your sisters take Aly along to help her prepare for tomorrow. I have business to discuss with Luca," he directs my oldest sister. I lean down and place a kiss on her cheek before Aria takes her hand, and the girls head upstairs.

Once we're in my father's office, he speaks again. "This girl is bad for your head," he says on a sigh like it pains him. "I honestly never expected you to fall in love. I thought one day I would arrange a marriage for you."

"Once we're married, it will be better."

My father sits back, his fingers steepled as he thinks. "You ready to go to war over this girl? Not even an heir will bring a truce now."

"Yes." I don't even hesitate.

"Very well." He stands up, and I mimic his actions. My father extends his hand to shake mine.

I leave the room with an overwhelmingly positive outlook. The notion that I'm suited for this life surrounds me. I've always felt in control with a gun in my hands, but following in my father's footsteps involves more than how precise I am with a target. I can't just be a born killer. It's what he's been trying to tell me most of my life, and I'm starting to see it now.

Coming down the stairs, I head outside. Vinny is there already, waiting for me.

"I need you to do some digging around for me." I keep my volume low, not wanting anyone to hear.

"Learn everything there is about Jonny Mancini. Find out how far he was willing to go to become boss. If he went to the trouble of faking his death, he's hiding more than that."

He nods. "Anything else?"

"Bring all of Aly's business stuff here. I want to be updated on what's been happening while she was away. Tell me if anyone has been sniffing around who shouldn't be. Do it discreetly."

He nods again and hesitates like he wants to say something else.

"Out with it," I tell him.

"Do you have a wedding gift for Aly?"

"I'm marrying her; isn't that a gift in itself?" I have no time for insignificant questions like this.

Vinny gives a low chuckle that makes me want to slap him across the head. Just because I'm getting married, it doesn't mean I'm getting soft. I might have to remind people of that.

He must see my expression and holds his hands out. "Let me explain, old friend."

I stay silent, expecting an explanation now.

"When I got married, I gave her a gold necklace. It was a small token the night before. It was my grandmother's, then she had something old for the wedding day. She thought it was sweet and repaid my kindness."

I grunt, walking away. Tomorrow, Aly Mancini will become Aly Rossi. I go stomping toward my range, needing to clear my head.

Aly

L UCA'S SISTERS ARE THE sweetest. The youngest one, Gia, does my hair as a practice trial for the wedding. It's beautiful. She is seriously talented with hair. Luna is painting my fingernails, while Katrina paints my toes.

"I knew Luca would eventually marry you," Gia says.

I wasn't expecting anyone to say that. "Why would you think that?"

"You were the only girl he would follow around," Luna adds in, sounding dreamy.

"He once put your face on his target. I knew then," Katrina says, laughing.

"We hated each other," I try to clarify.

"Naw, you were more like Romeo and Juliet. Luca just needed a justification to keep you," Aria responds. Gia is smiling, looking lovestruck as we talk about Luca and me.

"You realize they died in the end, right?" I question.

Aria merely shrugs, while Gia responds, "You both are too serious for your own good."

"What would you know about love?" Aria asks Gia.

She blushes, turning her head. "Nothing. My marriage was arranged when I was born. I'm not allowed to date." It doesn't sound convincing at all. Aria raises her eyebrow, making her sister shrink away.

I feel bad for her, so I add in, "I first met Luca when I was sixteen. But he also threatened to kill me." Shrugging, my mind instantly goes to that day. I can still see him perfectly. Those bright blue eyes that hold me captive.

"Couples that slay together, stay together?" Aria pipes in, laughing.

I smile, liking the saying, even though it's not accurate. Luca and I happen to be unlikely hearts who found each other. He's never let me down. He had the power to set the bar for me, even though we hated each other. Even amongst all that, I always believed he had a good soul. He's shown it to me in his unique way for years. He is the one man to ever make my heart race. At the start, I thought it was because I was frightened of him. My heart even raced when I thought about him. But soon I realized what I was feeling was anticipation.

CHAPTER 25

ALY

ONCE LUCA'S SISTERS LEAVE, I'm left alone to my thoughts. I have no idea if Luca will come back to his room tonight. I miss my mother. I'm starting to realize the girls who worked for me have become my friends, and I miss them. I'm lonely. Tomorrow will be my wedding day, and the only person there, truly for me, will be Luca.

This day has come up so fast I almost don't believe it, and my stomach flutters excitedly. Without a doubt, I want to marry Luca. I like the idea of us being like Romeo and Juliet, but in the end, we better get our happily ever after.

If my family were able to see that, maybe we could rewrite the future. Luca's family is accepting of it. Or maybe that's because they think they have the upper hand.

Resting my head on the window, I watch the stars high in the sky. Cars have been coming and going but don't stay long. I wonder what Luca is up to.

When I have given up on Luca coming to bed, our bedroom door opens. It doesn't have the force behind it as it normally does. I sit up, half expecting someone other than Luca.

He cockily walks in, wearing dress pants, his dress shirt wide open. His eyes are vibrant, telling me he's excited about something.

"You ready to become a Rossi?" he asks me. Keeping his eyes on me, he takes off his shirt, expecting a reply.

"I'm ready to become your wife and for everything that comes along with it."

I can't go back home anymore. That would be a death sentence. Becoming a Rossi has started to give me hope. I feel protected and love it here. His family has welcomed me with open arms. When it comes down to it, I feel cherished and special, a feeling I never want to let go of.

"I have a gift for you."

My eyes widen as I sit up in bed. Luca has never given me a gift before. "Why?"

He's standing shirtless, looking every bit as powerful as he is. He doesn't take my question lightly, and I watch as he forms his answer before replying.

"I wanted to show good faith in our marriage, in the team we will become. If I am to succeed in my plans, I need you to be strong by my side. I don't want a meek wife who lets me get away with everything. If I'm to stay strong, I need someone who's not scared of me, even when I may become frightening."

He's incredibly intense and passionate as he speaks, showing how strongly he believes in this. When Luca shows emotions, they are so powerful it seems to take over my heart. Like all those other times, it pulses with a ferocity. This is the Luca who believes in us, but if I ever betray him, this is also the side that wouldn't think twice about killing me. Because if I ever betray him, I would be ripping out his heart, and he would finish the job by killing his soul with my life.

"I love you." I wish I could show him how much. I wish there was a way to prove this isn't one-sided.

He comes down to the bed and forces his lips on mine. My nails scrape at his back, trying to get him closer, to prove I will never betray him. I need that skin to skin. It seems to be the only way to settle both of our hearts.

Our lips press together, our breaths becoming one. His weight crushes me against the bed. It's like we're battling for each other's heart. I bite his lip, my nails scraping down his back. He pushes his erection into me as he pulls my hair, moving my head wherever he wants it.

It feels like we're fighting for or against something. I'm just not a hundred percent sure what. Maybe we need this to confirm we both hold each other by the heart. One tiny squeeze and we have the power to ruin one another. Or maybe this is a warning of what will come if we destroy the trust we have somehow built up.

I hear his hiss when one of my nails scrapes a little too deep, and he takes my hands, moving them above my head, securing them with his.

He's pinned me down so I can't move. His legs hold mine too. I'm wearing a short, barely there nightgown with no panties. A light draft dances across my upper thighs, my nightgown having risen to my waist, exposing me to him. I push myself against him, unable to break free of his demanding kiss.

His lips come to my neck, kissing, sucking, and nipping. It's on the edge between hurting and feeling good, just like everything else we seem to do to each other.

When I look at him, I think he is the most handsome man I have ever seen. I love the seriousness of his features. Even his natural smile is menacing, where you can't tell if he's happy or not. I watch his face break, making his hard features become softer—still rigid, yet lighter.

I know right then that I will always follow Luca, no matter what. I gave my heart to him before I even realized it.

I try to move my hands; I want to touch his face, but he holds them tighter. He manages to pull down his pants and boxers to his thighs, then he's plunging into me.

I moan out, welcoming how amazing he feels inside me. He thrusts into me like he's punishing me. I keep up with him, moving with his body, meeting each of his hard movements.

He's taking my breast in, sucking ravishingly on it. I have no doubt I'll be marked in the morning. My whole body is bouncing with our quick pulses.

"Aly, you drive me mad," he grunts. I try to nip at him, wanting to rile him up. He groans as he goes so deep his stomach grinds against my clit with each of his punishing moves, and he hits the right spot. I scream out, my whole body shaking from the orgasm exploding out of me.

Luca makes two deep thrusts before moaning my name. It sounds primal and ferocious. If I didn't know him, it might scare me.

Lazily, he lets go of my hands, and they go around his neck.

"Was that my present?"

He laughs, and instantly I want to hear that sound every day of my life. It's sexy and makes my heart flutter. "No."

Slowly, he pulls out of me, removing my hands from around him. I miss the connection already.

"I'm giving you your business back."

I'm taken aback by the fact that he thinks he could take it away. But at the same time, I'm shocked, speechless, because he had been adamant he didn't want me to do that.

He places his fingers on my mouth. "I have your computer, and I have my guys making certain your girls are still safe and no one has tried to sweep in."

He's being sexist right now, but the thought is sweeter than hell. He knows this is important to me, and he's letting me do what I love. And I do love it.

"Thank you," I concede. It does mean a lot to me. I worked hard to get it up and running.

"Let's get some sleep. Tomorrow is going to be a busy day."

CHAPTER 26

ALY

I AWAKEN TO THE sound of Italian chatter from Cecilia and Violetta who helped me try on wedding dresses. The sun is just starting to hit me in the eyes, making me squeeze them tighter. With a groan, I roll over, hiding my face into the plush pillows. Breathing in, I can smell Luca on the sheets. My arm goes out, wanting to hide in his large frame, hoping to get a few additional minutes of sleep, but his side is already cold and vacant.

"We have your dress," Violetta singsongs. Along with being identical, their voices sound almost the same too. I can hear more of the blinds being opened, the vibrant pink and yellow sky shining through brightly.

"Up you go," I'm told. Huffing, I turn over, my eyes attempting to open. The sharp contrast of dark and light makes me blink a bunch of times before they can stay fully open.

A replica of the dress Luca cut off my body is hanging beautifully in the middle of the room. My lips immediately curve upward, remembering his face when he saw me in it. I knew he liked it.

My door opens again, and all of Luca's sisters come barreling in. Gia jumps on my bed, looking all dreamy. "You're getting married today!" The other three are standing around, already with dresses on. Pulling my covers to my neck, I remember I'm still very much naked underneath. They're all standing there, expecting me to get up.

"Ah, can you give me five to get dressed?" Everyone either smiles or snickers, but no one leaves. They simply turn their backs. No boundaries—got it.

Standing, I quickly put on panties and a bra before I slip on one of Luca's shirts and a pair of shorts.

"Done—" That's all I get out before the women all start talking amongst each other, while I'm shuffled to where they want me.

I'm nervous and jittery. With me never dating, I never thought about my wedding day. No one else ever spoke of it either. I don't have expectations for this day. As all the Rossi women crowd around me, determined to make me perfect, my heart pangs for my own mother. Growing up, she was my best friend. She should be here.

"Will my mom be in attendance?" I quietly ask Luca's mother as she puts my veil in place. All the other girls have left, needing to be at their designated spot, leaving the two of us alone.

Sympathy swarms her eyes as she says, "It was too much of a risk." She pauses, holding onto my hands. "You are becoming one of us now. Luca puts on a strong front, but he's had a hard life. You have the power to destroy him in ways no one else can. If you do that, I will destroy everything you love. It's the mother's job to protect what is hers, as it will be your job when you have children. Mafia women need to be resilient; we are the backbone that makes everything flow. Without us, the small details would crumble. The foundation of our empire would breakdown into nothing. Our job is the hardest, because there is little recognition, but it is also the most satisfying job there is. I will never take the place of your mother, but I will love you the same as all my children. I will protect everyone who comes under that umbrella." She lifts my veil and kisses me on both of my cheeks.

E VERYONE IS OUTSIDE WAITING for me. Luca's father offered to walk me down the aisle, but I declined. It didn't feel right. After all, I am giving myself away. I like the symbolism of it all. The doors open to their backyard, and music flows lightly around the grounds.

There is a lush green archway where Luca stands. Beautiful, delicate white flowers are dotted throughout. The grass is soft with each of my steps. White flower petals lead my way as I walk toward my soon-to-be husband.

The Rossi family all watch me, but I can't pull my eyes away from Luca. He's standing stiff but with a real smile poking its way through. His blue eyes pierce my soul; they shine with knowledge and warmth. He's breathtaking. Luca has no mask in place, showing his emotions as I walk toward him.

His suit fits him perfectly, stretching across his broad shoulders. I can already feel him pulling my heartstrings. With each step, he gets a better grasp on it. Tears shine in my eyes, and I'm taken aback by the emotion that clog my throat. I have to turn away for fear of crying.

Aria is standing up as my bridesmaid, and a man named Vinny is standing with Luca. The rest of the family is in the front row, as there are no others. There are no chairs. It's very intimate. As I come to the end of the aisle, Luca steps toward me, taking both my hands.

"You look amazing," he leans down and whispers in my ear.

The man in front of us begins the ceremony. "Luca, repeat after me. I, Luca Rossi, take thee, Aly Mancini..." The words fade to the background. I find myself still entranced with Luca. I note the pause at the obey part, and Luca puts pressure on my hand, reassuring me. His eyes crinkle. It all makes it sound like I'm Luca's property. I keep telling myself the words are not what's important. It's the fact that we love each other, and will honor each other, 'til death do us part.

Luca is staring at me, his words sounding every bit as serious as his face looks. His tone is strong and clipped.

"Aly, repeat after me."

I nod. My voice doesn't carry as well as Luca's when I say my part. My hands tremble, but not because I'm scared. They tremble at what a big deal this is to me. Seeing Luca take this seriously makes me love him even more.

"I now pronounce you man and wife," the officiate says.

Luca steps into me, seizing my shoulders, and kisses me. His lips mold to mine, his tongue sweeping in as he tilts my body into a dip. Bringing me up, he leans in. "I love you," he murmurs before we turn toward his family standing out in the yard.

Flutes of champagne are handed out, and everyone cheers for our new union. Luca and I cheers, our glasses clinking together. He still hasn't lost his seriousness. After taking our sips, he takes my drink, passing it on to one of his sisters. His hand splays down my back, leading the way before he begins dancing with me. He's a talented dancer, much better than me. He holds me strong as he moves us in smooth, elegant movements. It feels perfectly natural to be in his arms. Placing my head on his chest, his heart thumping heavier than normal, I allow myself to get lost in our bubble. It's my favorite place to be when nothing else matters but us.

By the time we finish, his family has taken a seat, watching us. There are a few round tables off to the side, where we will be having our lunch. Luca leads me to the tables, placing me beside Vinny's wife.

He stands, shaking Luca's hand, before they step away to have a conversation I can't hear.

"I'm Salem," Vinny's wife introduces herself. "I've been told I'm your new best friend." Her voice is sweet. She and Vinny are the only nonfamily invited.

"Did Vinny say that because he's best friends with Luca?" I ask, taking a sip of my drink.

"Luca informed me the day after he bought you flowers. Sorry we're just meeting now." She means well, and I smile at her.

Part of me wants to fight it and demand that Luca can't determine who my best friend will be. I shut down my insecurities, believing my husband means well, but I hate feeling like I'm being controlled.

"Cheers." I raise my glass to hers. I have to remind myself I have gained family and friends by marrying Luca. I'm so used to being by myself that I forget what it's like to have so many people around. Everyone is trying to be helpful and welcoming. I should feel blessed.

Luca doesn't seem happy with what Vinny is telling him. They stomp toward the house, leaving me alone with everyone else. I wonder if this is what his mom meant in a roundabout way. That I have to be flexible and understanding of their world. That even in times like my wedding, Luca can't just be with me. He needs to share himself with everyone.

V INNY BETTER HAVE A solid reason why he pulled me away.
"We have a problem," he starts as soon as we're far enough away to not be heard.

"Yeah?"

"I need to show you."

"I'm not leaving Aly alone. We just got married," I say, exasperated that he would even ask.

"You need to see this." He stands firm. I resist the urge to pinch the skin between my eyes. I want one day where I get to enjoy life with my new bride.

Aly is with Salem, and I feel more confident in leaving her alone. Aly needs a friend outside of the family, like what I have with Vinny. I'm happy they are getting along.

"Show me then." I stomp back toward the house when I would rather be enjoying the day with my wife.

A box is on the table, and Vinny points to it. I open it up, and it's lined with plastic and blood. Opening the lid farther, there is no question that the parts in the box belong to my cousin Pauly. The family ring still on his finger confirms it.

I should have killed him when he let Aly out of sight. Instead, I've been too busy entertaining her and not allowing her to leave my view. Who knows what they were able to torture out of him? I wonder if this is a sign that someone has found out that she is my weakness, or if it's the Mancinis sending a message; maybe it's a little of both.

Even with all these thoughts, the guilt starts to creep up. I try not to acknowledge it. My heart is racing, and I have to control my breathing. Have my actions led to my cousin's death? Just like when I was young and my friends were killed in front of me? It reminds me all over again why I married Aly. I am taking away something Mancini loves and making it mine.

CHAPTER 27

ALY

LUCA HAS BEEN WORKING long hours since the day of our wedding. I've been informed that we have an engagement party that will become a surprise wedding reception in the next couple of days. Once again, I'm helpless in that he's making all the decisions, and I'm the wife who waits for him.

I overhear some of the men talking about all the big Italian families being invited. Hope blossoms in my chest. Maybe this is the start of the Mancinis and Rossis making amends. Maybe this means I won't have to be cooped up in the mansion. I can start coming and going as I please.

"Aly."

I stop typing on my laptop when Luca comes into the room. His demeanor is stiff, causing me to worry.

"What's wrong?" I stand up immediately. Luca is always so abrupt, but this is different.

"How are your girls?" he asks, referring to my business. He has probably already placed a bunch of stuff on my computer, so he knows what I was doing. I'm not some naïve girl who thinks he gave me everything back and wouldn't be checking in on me. Maybe he noticed the email in my spam. Another email telling me it would soon be my time. But time for what?

"They're good," I say cautiously.

He tilts his head, scrutinizing my answer like he doesn't trust my response. Then he nods before he walks around his room.

"Why do you stay in here, when you could be out?"

"No reason other than I like your window." I like watching the comings and goings of the house and the way the sun shines brightly into his room when the curtains are held back. "Can I go to my office?" I ask.

"My men can take you." It still seems like something is on his mind and he's struggling to say it. "I also got word that your mother is sick."

My heart jumps into my throat. "I need to go to her." I'm already gathering up all the things I need from the room.

"It could be a trap." Luca's voice is soft. "My men will go in with you to be sure."

"Why don't you come with me?"

His hands cup my face. "I wish I could. I have too much work." He kisses me on the forehead, but his lips are cold. They don't have the warmth they did a day ago. It worries me.

"Is that how you kiss your wife?"

A deep, low chuckle leaves him, and I bask in its sound. His hands tug me in, so my chest hits his torso, and he mashes his lips against mine. It's strong and commanding. The way he kisses me leaves no doubt in my mind that he loves me. It settles my heart and stomach as I cling to the connection we share.

"Call me when you're on your way home. I want to have dinner with you tonight, away from my family."

It's amazing how I can go from being uncertain to knowing everything is right in the world by the smallest bit of his affection.

He starts walking out but stops and comes back to me, placing another kiss on my lips. It's like he can't get enough of me. When we're together, I'm all he sees, then when he's gone for too long, it's like he forgets I'm here waiting for him.

'M STUCK IN THE middle of the backseat with three bodyguards and a driver. The men do not talk to me or one another. It's boring and suffocating. When my mother's home comes into view, we pull to a stop, and they step out, sweeping the area before they give me the okay to leave the car.

The nurses smile at me as soon as I walk in. "I'm so sorry I haven't visited on my normal days," I say as I sign in. "How is my mother?"

Writing out my name, I pause, waffling on which last name to write, since it's not common knowledge that I've been married.

From behind, the head nurse walks in. "Aly." She pauses, and my eyes come up from having written down just **Aly**. "You are no longer on the pre-approved guest list."

My heart stills. "What?" I'm the one person who visits her. The nurse gives nothing away, her face emotionless. I have had many warm conversations with her, so I'm confused as to where this is coming from.

"You are no longer allowed to be on the premises. I must ask you to leave." For a brief moment, sympathy shines before it's swept away, making me unsure if I had seen it at all.

"She needs company. She gets sick less when she's not lonely."

"Rest assured, her being sick is not from being lonely. She has been receiving the same number of visiting hours as normal with your absence." It feels like she's accusing me of being a bad daughter because I haven't been around. I had no choice.

"Who said I couldn't come in? She's my mother and needs me."

"That does not matter. Now leave."

"Will she be okay?"

"I'm sorry. I cannot give you that type of information."

I'm on the verge of tears. I miss my mother so badly, and hearing she is sick... What if the last time I visited her was my last?

"Let me see her for one minute," I plead.

She picks up the phone, asking for security. I don't want to leave, but I'm being moved out the doors by Luca's men. My feet drag on the ground as I try to keep their hands off my arms. One second, I'm fighting my own security; the next, I search behind me, hoping maybe by some miracle I'll see my mother. I go back and forth as my heart hurts that I can't visit the woman who raised me with all of her love. Dropping her whole life, for me to have a chance at one.

I keep trying to free myself of their grasp but can't. The guards are too strong for me. I'm placed in the back like a child having a tantrum, the doors child locked, keeping me in place. The car leaves the parking lot, my opinion unimportant. Crossing my arms over my chest, I stew over the situation that unfolded. A tear springs loose, and I wipe it away with my palm. All I wanted was to see my mother. Proving to myself that she is healthy and not growing worse by the day. The worry that grows deep in my chest won't remove itself until I lay eyes on her. Dread and guilt over not being with her claw into me, and nothing will make it go away until she is in front of me.

When we stop next, we're in front of my "yoga studio." The men follow me like before. "I need a moment alone."

"Luca said not to let you out of our sight," one of the bodyguards says, keeping his head straight.

"Of course he did." I unlock the doors and walk in. Nothing has changed since I was here last. Yet, I feel different.

Sitting down at my desk, I allow my tears to come instead of forcing them away. I don't hold back, not caring who hears. I miss my mom. I'm worried for her health and don't think I would be able to ever get over it if my last time visiting her was the final time. She has been my rock, my "person," my whole life. My body shakes, frightened that I may never get to see her again. I have this feeling like she may not make it. She has been getting increasingly worse each year.

My stomach rolls with nausea at the turmoil that runs through me. Part of me doesn't know who to blame. Do I blame myself?

Luca for stealing me away. Or my father for hurting me as much as I've probably hurt him.

My yoga studio phone rings, and I ignore it, unable to control my quivering voice. When it rings a second time, I take a deep breath, trying to calm my heart but never settling it. "Hello?" I answer. The men's ears perk up, watching my every move. Turning in my chair, I put my back toward them.

"Hello, daughter," my father's deep, cold voice is heard on the other end of the line. I swallow the lump in my throat that wants to break free. "Do not say a word."

Talking to my father now is wrong, but he also holds the key to my mother. My heart begins to pound in my chest. I hear footsteps shuffling, and my heart beats stronger. I try to hold onto the phone without showing my slight tremble, but it's impossible. My hand still shakes more than I would like.

"Sorry, we're not starting any new yoga classes anytime soon. Please check back on our website for when classes may start again," I say when one of the men walk in front of me, eyeing me like I'm doing something wrong.

"We will meet soon, Aly," he says before he even has a chance to tell me the real reason for his call. I hang up, my body hot and beginning to sweat.

Chapter 28

Luca

E VERYTHING IS COMING TOGETHER. Our "engagement party" is all set up, with every important don and family coming, just as I knew they would. They all want to see whose family is stronger than the other.

I can't wait to see Mancini's face when he realizes his daughter loves me and chooses the Rossis over him. It will be the ultimate revenge for my family. My father will be able to show everyone that he is smarter than Mancini, and that I, the adopted son who everyone looked down upon, is now one of them and better at it than they are. This is retaliation for Mancini killing my two innocent friends, my cousin Pauly, and everything he has done to my family.

Coming into my bedroom, I watch Aly put on a pair of earrings I gave her. She's stunning in a white dress that dips so low in the back you can see the dimples that sit above her ass. It wraps around her neck and dips just low enough in the front to make you want to see more. She is stunning. Her dark hair has a slight wave to it, and she is wearing bright red lipstick.

Coming in from behind, I place my chin on her shoulder, staring at the two of us in her mirror. My olive skin is a complete contrast to her pale, creamy flesh. "I want everyone to see how much I love you tonight," I say in a low, gravelly voice. I'm honestly getting everything I ever wanted. I couldn't be happier. I even find my lips tilting up higher than normal and laughing. I no longer have the urge or compulsion to stalk and kill like I had before. She has grounded me in a way I never thought possible.

"You are stunning." I turn to give her a soft kiss on the cheek. She smiles at me, but the brightness in her eyes has dimmed. I've been waiting for her to bring up the fact that she wasn't allowed to see her mother, but she hasn't. Part of me is disappointed that she hasn't confided in me. But our relationship is still young. We have the rest of our lives to grow with each other.

I plan to give her another gift after the world learns she is mine. I have been able to make some moves so her mother will be able to come live here. It has not gone unnoticed how important she is to her, and I want her to be happy. I can't wait to give her the good news. Although, I doubt Mancini will go down without a fight once he realizes I have stolen his mistress away from him too.

"Ready?"

She turns toward me. "As ready as I'll ever be." There is a shakiness to her voice that I don't like. But I try to understand. Tonight is when she will do her final stand against her family. I can't imagine what must be going through her head.

"You will be safe no matter what." I try to ease her mind, kissing her on the forehead. I hold her in my arms, loving how she fits perfectly, like the lost piece I had no idea was missing.

Aly

THE BACK OF THE limo is dark and cold. My nerves are splitting while Luca appears calm beside me, his arm around my shoulders. I can't get warm, even with Luca's heat radiating into me. I wish I could be as unaffected as him. When I look up at his shadowed face, I instantly feel love for him. Tonight, I'll be forced to face my father, and facing him terrifies me. His retaliation to the news I've married Luca frightens me to the core. I have become incredibly entangled with the two families, and I feel like they're both pulling me down like seaweed. It's hard to keep my breath, when each time I move, the harder each one pulls. But then Luca gazes down, and it's like he's breathing life into me, but it only lasts for a brief second. If I sink too far, will Luca be able to save me?

I hadn't realized that I was staring at his chiseled jaw until his hand cups my cheek, the rough pad of his thumb stroking my soft skin, as he asks, "You finding the answers you're looking for?"

His features are sharper than normal with his five o'clock shadow. I remember seeing him and being so intimidated once upon a time. I tried not to show how frightened I was of him. Now, he is nothing short of gorgeous. He's tender—and vicious, but I'm no longer scared. I like seeing his two sides. It reminds me of a strong man, who no one dares to go against, but get him alone, and he is the most loving person there is. He feels deeply, his emotions running high. His refusal of allowing it to be seen heightens it when he does allow what is going through him to be apparent.

"You'll always love me no matter what, right?" I ask. His fingers cup my jaw. He's searching my face, probably trying to determine what I'm thinking.

"I never let go of what's mine. You will be a part of me 'til death."

It's his way of trying to show me how far his love goes. The limo stops, and I take a deep breath. When we walk in, everyone in this room will know Luca kidnapped me, but the real show will be me proving to them that I love him.

"'Til death do us part," I repeat our wedding vow and lean in to kiss his lips. This kiss is chaste and unlike all our other kisses. Luca's only signal that he is just as nervous about tonight as I am.

The twenty steps to the main doors seem like a mile. We are both quiet and on edge. Luca opens the door, music floating toward us. Every single eye is on us, with the guests already seated at their tables.

The lump in my throat sticks as I attempt to swallow. Every important family is here. Tension in the air is high. Excitement gleams in everyone's eyes, but I don't think it's to celebrate our so-called engagement. I suspect that once the real news is announced, the "party" will truly begin.

Luca squeezes my hand as we step forward together, united. Searching the faces, I find my father. His eyes are narrowed at our hands being intertwined. He's always had the power to intimidate me. I can't help but feel like a young child, even though I'm an adult.

Luca leads me to the dance floor with our audience and pulls me in close. Being protected in his arms, I can breathe easier. The rest of the room is silent. A pin dropping would be heard, even over the music. My ears are on alert, listening for anything that doesn't sound right. Luca's men are also watching the crowd, with a close eye on my father to guarantee everything goes well.

"Try to relax and enjoy our moment. No one matters but the two of us." His low, husky voice is at my ear, and he nips my lobe, making me smile. Taking a deep breath, I try to will myself to relax. I try to forget about the hundreds of people watching us.

The song ends, and Luca dips me, much like he did on our wedding day. Just like that day, he lays his lips on mine. The open affection startles me, but my body welcomes his touch. It responds in habit of kissing him back. I can hear the gasps from around the room, some chairs scraping against the floor.

When Luca brings me upright, I'm breathless. This man can kiss. I could do it all night. I've easily gotten lost in him just from a single touch of his lips. My skin flushes, realizing we are on display. My father is standing at the edge of the dance floor, his face red and angry.

His aggravation has never been directed at me before. Still holding my hand, Luca is leading me to the podium. This is the moment. The moment I am most afraid of.

"Good evening," Luca greets everyone, his voice steady and strong. "Aly and I are incredibly blessed to have you all attend our special evening."

We watch over the crowd, becoming aware that the truth is about to come out in the next second.

"Instead of an engagement celebration—" Here it comes. My eyes sweep the crowd once more, finding my father. Every muscle in his body is rigid, ready to strike like a snake. Coy is now beside him, equally angry. "We are celebrating a union blessed by God. Please welcome my new bride, Aly Rossi!" He kisses me again, his lips strong. My body shakes, unsure how the crowd will receive our news.

Braking apart, the Mancini side have all stood up, but no weapons have been drawn yet. They were probably all taken away before they could enter. Wise—I have no doubt there would be a gun show in here.

On the opposite side of my father is Luca's dad. He's smug, his eyes right on his enemy, my father. My stomach rolls like I'm going to be sick. Deep down, I hoped our wedding could become a truce, but right now, all I can see is revenge from the two major Italian dons in the area. It's now I realize that I will only ever be a causality of war.

My chest rises and falls, my eyes casting down with the roar of my blood rushing through me. The crowd is silent, waiting for someone to applaud or do something. All eyes bounce between us and our fathers, waiting to see if they make a move. The pressure builds in me, and I need to escape. I take a step back. Luca's hand slides behind my back, pulling me beside him, refusing to let me go. Slow clapping begins, starting at Luca's father and trickling into the crowd. The fake smile on my face hurts as I expect some sort of retaliation. It frightens me to the core, knowing my father refuses to lose and the fallout from that.

Luca says a few more words before he leads me back down onto the dance floor. The moment his grasp loosens, I escape, needing to be away from all eyes. Turning to the side toward a door, my hands slap it as I push it open. Luca is on my heels; I can feel him with me, and noise begins in the ballroom. Breaking away from the ballroom, I see an open garbage can. Running toward it, I throw up everything I've eaten today. He stands, holding my hair, his other hand circling my bare back.

It feels too kind, when I've embarrassed him, making the situation worse.

"We need to go back in there, and I may have to do some business now that the news has been given."

Work. Everything is work; every action is something for the family. I'm starting to realize you can never do anything for yourself. It's always what's good for the family.

"Luca." My father's voice comes from behind us, along with a bunch of other footfalls. "You have stolen from me once again."

My husband stands up straight, unafraid. He's never afraid.

"I was hoping you would see it as gaining a capable son." His voice is laced with danger and hatred.

"Are the rumors true—you killed Jonny when he came out of hiding to protect his sister?"

"I don't think my wedding reception is the time for that type of business."

Luca takes my hand and drags me back to the party. My head is swimming. The other dons come and give their congratulations one at a time while handing us an envelope of money for a gift.

"You look like you need a drink," Salem says as she takes a seat beside me, and I watch Luca greet the men who take all his attention.

Even though I've met Salem recently, I feel like we have a connection and she is someone I can trust. Leaning my head on her shoulder for a split second, I respond, "You must have read my mind."

"Well, you are the talk of the night," she tells me. I don't think she's referring to the fact that this is my wedding reception.

"Come on." She stands, tilting her head toward the open bar.

Even as the bride, we have to fight our way to the front. I order a vodka soda, needing something harder to deal with all the emotions running rampant in me.

"You okay? You're a little pale."

I touch her arm. "I just need some fresh air and a moment alone."

"I'll cover for you." She nods toward the one bodyguard who is practically glued to me. She walks up to him and hands him our drinks. "We need to go to the ladies' room." Then she walks away, and I follow. As soon as we round the corner, we take off running.

With the help of my friend, we find an exit that leads to the side of the building. "I'll meet you at the bathrooms, and we can walk in together," I tell her, escaping into the night.

The air is chilly but refreshing. It allows me to take a deep breath and hold it in my lungs before I let it go. Tilting my head up, the stars shine bright, reminding me that I'm a speck in the universe. The thought helps calm my nerves, knowing there are more important things happening in the world than my marriage.

"Have I ever wronged you, Aly?" I recognize it's my father beside me before he steps into the light and shows himself. "I thought respecting your mother's wishes was for the best. But now..." I turn to him. He's sighing and shaking his head. "It seems I was wrong. You've tarnished the Mancini name. If you were anyone else, I would put a bullet in your chest. Did I not love you enough?"

"It has nothing to do with your love. I love him."

His head rears back like I have slapped him. "You need to choose. It's Luca or your mother." His voice is eerily calm and smooth, making goose bumps skate over my skin. "I've been to see her, and she is asking for you, but the doctors don't think she will live past this year."

Guilt eats at me. The nausea sits deep in my stomach. "Come back to me, Aly, and all will be forgotten." He grabs my hand, placing a kiss on my knuckles.

"I've already said my vows."

"They mean nothing until there is an heir." His voice grows stronger, and I can tell he's trying not to lose his temper with me. He slips something into my palm and then closes my fingers around it before kissing my fingers.

"I will be coming for you, daughter. Luca's fate lands on you now." When he lets go of my hand, I open it up. A clear vial sits heavy. "If Luca still lives tomorrow night, I will know your answer."

He steps away, opening the door just as one of Luca's men barges through it. He takes in my father and me, causing my dad to laugh as he walks away.

"We have her. She is safe," I hear my bodyguard say.

He grabs my arm, his fingers biting into my skin. With a yank, I free myself, stomping away. I go a few steps before Luca is storming his way toward us. My fingers are clenched around the vial my father gave me. I have nowhere to put it; I'm not even wearing a bra.

Luca grasps my shoulders when he meets me. "Are you okay?" His eyes are trailing down my body, inspecting me, his worried eyes crinkling around the edges.

"I'm fine. I just needed a moment to myself."

"You mean a moment with your father." He's staring at my face, searching for my truth.

"He ended up outside too, yes. Can you broker a truce of some sort? Can't the families learn to work together?"

"The bad blood is too thick for that." He pauses, nodding his men off. "Are you ready to go back out there?" He offers me his hand, the one time he hasn't just taken it. Taking a step forward, I begin walking refusing his hand. My head tilts up in necessary defiance, and Luca matches my steps.

I want to see my mother so badly, but having to give up Luca doesn't seem right. The poison in my hand is like a ticking bomb. I don't have it in me to kill him, and I never could. I truly love Luca. I fell in love with him years ago.

Stepping into the beautiful ballroom, Luca begins to lead me to the dance floor. His steps are slightly ahead of mine. The room still has the unbearable tension as before.

CHAPTER 29

LUCA

MY HEART RICOCHETS IN my chest as I wait for Aly to tell me what she's holding. With each sweep to hold her hand, she takes a step away, leaving her out of my grasp. Her feet falter for a brief second when she sees I'm guiding her toward the dance floor. There will be no hiding from me there. My chest drums, hoping I'm reading her wrong. It's not that I don't trust her; I don't trust her father. Tomorrow, some of my men will be fired for losing her, if I'm feeling generous.

Loud chatter envelops the room. Everyone is shaking hands, smiling, but the underlying tension remains. With each stride we take, more eyes land on us. The lights seem brighter than they did a moment ago. All I want is to hold her, to breathe her in. I need her to calm my heart in a way only she can. Using all my restraint, I allow her to have the space she seems to be clinging to. Each muscle in my body is rigid, becoming tight with her refusal to seek my touch out.

Stepping onto the dance floor, I turn toward her. Her eyes bounce around nervously, making my stomach slip further with the realization that we may not have the trust we need. There is still a light of hope that I'm wrong. I keep trying to convince myself as I position us to dance by placing one hand against the soft skin of her back, while my other hand grabs her fisted one that refuses to open.

My instinct is to crush her small hand until she is left with no other choice but to let whatever she is holding fall from her grasp. Instead, I pry her fingers from her palm with no effort, even with her using all her strength. I slide my palm over hers, our fingers interlocking. The cylinder resting between our hands. It's cold and hard, matching my stance as I hold her. My heart splinters more as we stand in the middle of the room, and she has yet to attempt to explain. Her eyes are wide, going from her hand to my eyes. I thought she resuscitated my black heart to something that may be considered living, but it breaks each second my wife, the woman I love, refuses to meet my eye. The betrayal tastes bitter on my tongue, cracking my chest with what feels like a baseball bat pounding into me.

With elegance, I spin her around the floor, masking all of my emotions. "Little bird, are you trying to escape your cage?"

All this time, I've been worried about my actions hurting her—not that she would try to hurt me. Her father called her while she was at her studio; I should have confronted her then. Have they been plotting this the whole time? Am I the one they've been laughing at? Gazing down at her, all I can see is her father in her. It sickens me to think I've been played so perfectly. That I allowed myself to love, only for it to be a mirage of what my life could never be.

My chest aches in a way I have never felt before. I've never allowed myself to get attached. I have tried to stay emotionless because, in the end, no one can hurt you if you don't care. But with her held in my arms, I feel that gut-stabbing hurt of treachery. That sick feeling is on repeat. My body feels love, but my mind is more cautious. It takes all my strength not to walk off this floor, to escape this nauseating feeling that sits like a rock in my gut.

Holding her hand tighter, I spin her out from me, then pull her back in, this time opening her hand enough to see a small cylinder, much like a perfume sample, with liquid inside.

"You will drink that." My voice is hoarse and raspy, and it pains me to say the words. Her body has a visible shake to it, and she pales. Tears form in her eyes as she realizes she's been caught. She displays the typical cowardly signs, and I thought at least she would hold her ground and keep her chin up.

"I can't." Her words hardly escape her pretty parted lips, and I have to lean in to hear her. She's had time to come clean, to confide in me, to trust me. But like everyone else in my life, except my father, she never believed in me, in us. We could have been amazing together.

I hold her stronger. She swallows twice, her arm trying to escape my hold. Her efforts are wasted as I hold her in place.

"No one will come to you. Remember I was the one who saved you," I remind her, prying her hand open again. We have stopped dancing, but our chests are pressed together. Her heart beats rapidly, matching mine. Her refusal to defend herself further spikes my frustrations and anger. Her mouth opens and closes, yet not a sound can be heard.

I should have known better than to allow myself to fall in love. In the end, everyone leaves me. I thought she could be different.

"I wasn't going to use it." There is begging in her tone, and it sounds ugly coming from her mouth as she starts to defend herself. It's the pathetic tone everyone has the moment they realize they are going to die.

"Don't start lying to me now."

It hurts me to do this. I'm holding her hand that's trying to get away from me, but I can't fully move it. Not because I can't, but because my heart is having a hard time letting her go. Inch by inch, I force my hand to move hers up, the poison coming closer to those beautiful lips I loved to kiss.

A flicker of realization that I won't back down passes over her eyes. I wish there was another way. Her chest works double-time with short pants. She refuses to look around, making me live the horror of killing the one person I thought I could love.

Aly

I HOLD MY HUSBAND'S eyes, and the old feeling of being scared of him reappears. His jaw is tense, and his eyes are the deepest, darkest blue I've ever seen. He has this maddening expression chiseled into his sharp features like he wants to hurt me as badly as I've hurt him. There is pure hatred carved there. I try to step away from his hold, but he firmly holds me in place. I should have never taken the vial from my father. I should have been stronger. I wanted to see my mother and keep my marriage. I was greedy, and this is the consequence.

I try to focus on my breathing, to attempt to explain. I want to tell him the truth; it's on the tip of my tongue. With each attempt, my chest inflates, but it's like I've lost the ability to talk. I'm forced to live the moment Luca stops loving me. I watch his already hateful eyes glass over, and he looks at me like I'm nothing. I'm nothing more than a casualty in his world. The agonizing pain that shreds my insides is worse than death.

I try to turn away, not being able to watch him turn into a monster that lurks silently in men like him. His hold is iron-clad on my hand, slowly moving it up to my lips. I'm still lost, hoping to see a glimmer of the boy I know and the man I've fallen in love with. Part of me wants to drink the poison, to prove my loyalty to him. I was always brought up that loyalty is worth more than love. Love won't keep you alive and out of trouble, but loyalty can. I never believed it until now.

The entrance doors fly open, severing Luca's and my contact. Screams and hysteria erupt with blue uniforms invading our party. Luca's eyes are searching the room. I follow his watchful eyes to see them land on his sisters closest to the entrance.

His hold goes limp. "Family always comes first, Luca," he mutters to himself.

He looks back at me, and with a disgusted snarl, he drops my hand and takes a step away, leaving me standing in the middle of the room. I can't find the strength to go to my father, knowing it's wrong. He would think I was coming back for all the wrong reasons. Instead, I turn to find the same door that indirectly chooses my family over my husband. No one takes notice as police swarm the room. Taking one last glance over my shoulder, I see Luca is with his family. It's clear I'm no longer a part of that.

Leaving the ballroom, the hallway is vacant. Among the hollers and stomping in the other room, it's silent back here. Creepily silent. Picking up my pace, I run down the hall, my hands landing on the door to exit as a bag is whipped over my head.

My neck is pulled back before the rest of my body follows. It takes seconds for me to realize what's happening before I'm able to fight back. My feet are picked up as I thrash around, my efforts futile as I'm being carried away. The uneven movements carry me away, the door slamming shut, meeting the cold night's air. Each time I try to scream, the cord at the bottom of the bag is pulled tighter around my neck, making it hard to breathe. The realization that I have burned every bridge in my life does not go unnoticed by me. No one will be searching for me. I'm still the lost mafia princess no one wants.

CHAPTER 30

LUCA

C HAOS ERUPTS EVERYWHERE, AIDING in the ruin of the one night I honestly wanted for myself. I can't think too deeply into the betrayal of my wife, because I'm off running to help my family escape the embarrassment of tonight's events. Some of our relatives are handcuffed and hauled away. It's distressing to see your family arrested during one of our parties. It's not that it's uncommon to have the police up our asses, but we have enough on our side that they don't blindside us—on my wedding reception day no less. The whole scene that unfolds is bad business that will put a sour taste in the other families' mouths.

Amongst getting my sisters out safely, I lost track of Aly. I hate myself for trying to keep tabs on her while I have bigger problems I needed to handle. There will come a time when I will see her again and remind her of her actions.

Back at home, I pace the floor, sensing something is off. Being my father's top man, I need to be included in all of the meetings. I can't be dealing with how I want retribution against Aly. I'm stomping out mini fires from all the major families who think we have disgraced them.

"Luca, you're going to wear a hole in the carpet. We should have expected something like this. All the big families were in one place," says my father.

I nod before turning around to keep moving, trying to put my finger on what's bothering me. My gut is telling me it's not as simple as what my father says. I have an intense, overpowering feeling like something is wrong and I've missed a crucial piece of evidence.

I keep pushing Aly out of my mind; she isn't what's important right now. I trust my men to stay on her. There was no time to call them off, and I'm not the type to let someone like her slip through my fingers. She will get what's coming to her. Even with me wanting to pour poison down her throat, I don't want anyone else to touch what's mine. If I'm honest with myself, I could have never gone through with it all. The police barging in allowed me to pussy out and run away from my problem.

She makes me weak. I've never had a problem killing anyone. I blame my temporary hesitation on the shock of her deception. Sadness creeps into me, realizing she isn't who I thought she was. I was stupid to believe that love could conquer all. The mafia lifestyle doesn't allow for happy endings. You have clips of it, but that's it. Everyone has a number with a time when they will go out. Most will say it is too soon. No one dies of old age in my lifestyle; it is just a matter of time.

Stopping, I squeeze my eyes closed, feeling like I'm on the verge of a breakthrough. It's on the cusp of my mind; I can almost see it. Bringing my hand up, my fingers press into my forehead like it will help push my thought in front of me.

Vinny barges into our meeting, heaving out of breath. I spin toward him, annoyed my thought process was broken.

"We lost her." He gasps, holding onto the door handle, his body completely exerted.

"You lost who?" I ask, grinding my molars. Pushing my shoulders back, I try to alleviate the tension pinching them.

"Aly, boss."

My instinct is to bring my gun up and shoot my best friend, but he wasn't in charge of her. "Shoot whoever was supposed to tell me the news, then kill the guard on duty." I don't think twice about giving the orders.

"One more thing." He hesitates before turning to leave. I give him my full attention, waiting for him to continue. "Her father is searching for her. They know she's not here."

I want to rage, throw things, unload the clip in my gun, but I remain emotionless on the outside. Her father doesn't have her. He's either overconfident that Aly would do his dirty work, or he has someone in our house selling him information. I nod for Vinny to go, trying to keep my composure when I feel like my insides are exploding with irritation.

The door closes, and the room filled with Rossi men stays quiet, before I roar, "I need my wife back!" Frustration claws at me. I was stupid to let her go. She is my problem to deal with. My regret is not pulling her out by her hair and tying her down on my bed to do as I wish. It would have been well worth the cost to have her father watch his daughter being dragged away for disobeying me. It's that fire and defiance in her eyes that made me fall in love with her, and this time, I abandoned her. We both knew she wouldn't just smile and be pretty. Calming myself, I take a seat, annoyed I allowed everyone in this room to see me and everything I'm feeling. I should have never put myself on show for all to see.

My father is silent, thinking things through. For a quiet, soft-spoken man, he may seem harmless, but it's all an act to deceive.

"Put on extra guards. If Mancini believes we don't have his daughter, there is no stopping him from starting a war in our yard," my father announces.

My instincts kick in, and all I want to do is shoot and kill. My fingers are on fire with the need to pull a trigger. Adrenaline courses through me in a way that's never burned before. It's hard to be stoic when I'm anything but.

Aly's face sears into my mind like a freight train. I will kill everyone who is associated with the person who took her. If they hurt one hair on her head, their family will pay for their defiance. When Aly bleeds, it will be because of me. I would much rather her die from my hands than someone else's; that is how messed up my heart is.

"How do we know she's not just hiding out?" one of my uncles questions.

It's like her blood flows through mine.

It always has.

I can still feel it right now.

Ever since I met her, I felt this intense connection. I always had an internal response when something was wrong. It's why I ended up seeing her so often. My body wouldn't allow me to ignore its pestering compulsion to save her.

My chest constricts like someone is compressing it. She's not hiding out.

"Get the surveillance video before someone else gets their hands on it." Standing, I walk to my father, picking up his hand to kiss it.

I can no longer sit idle in this room. I need to do something to feel useful. I will not let my wife's blood spill because I sat back and did nothing.

Aly

SITTING IN A DARK room, my arms and legs are bound. The hard rope cuts into my soft skin. I'm parched. My lips are dry and pinch like they're cracking. Time has slipped away from me. I haven't seen anyone's face. They must have already started to plot their demands. If they were going to kill me for no reason, I would already be dead.

For the first time since I was sixteen, Luca isn't here to save me. Even if there was no threat and I was just nervous, he always showed up throughout the years. I never had a reason to be afraid, I learned. But now, the unfamiliar feeling of being terrified ripples through me. I sit here long enough to worry that I'll never get a chance to make everything right.

Luca will go on living and thinking that I betrayed him. He will use the hatred of believing that I used him, to drive his ambition. It frightens me to think what that will do to him. Men like Luca need a woman's love. It keeps the demons that prey on men who have nothing else to live for, away in the deep darkness of their souls. Turning them into monsters that even the devil doesn't want to keep.

I try to stay awake, but every so often, sleep takes me under. I lose track if it's day or night—if it has been one day or ten. Occasionally, I will wake with bread on my shoulder. The only way to eat it is by lifting my shoulder and hoping my mouth can latch onto it. The first time, it dropped to the floor, and I had to go without.

CHAPTER 31

LUCA

I SEARCH EVERYWHERE AND interrogate each man on duty. I search her computer, home, and yoga studio for any clues. Three threatening emails are found, but it all came from entitled street shits who think they're gangsters, because the school has suspended them a couple of times. When that becomes pointless, I begin investigating her father once again.

Pierre Mancini is crying too loudly, using his hierarchy to pull more allies to him. He's complaining that I've disrespected him by having his daughter disappear. Calling the truce we never had "broken." He's trying to place shame on our family, hoping our alliances won't stay faithful to us. He's smart to use this to his advantage if he knows his daughter is safe. But if he doesn't have her, he leaves no room for anyone to keep her alive. They could easily frame our family for it. Her death will cause gunfire in the streets. Either way, he has the advantage right now.

Everyone, including Mancini, comes up clean. My teeth grit across each other painfully, the tension in my shoulders rolling down my body in waves. I haven't slept in days. My eyes are sore but refuse to close with my mind continually working. I keep circling back to when the cops swarmed in and I lost my focus. The cameras mysteriously not working adds to all my problems. No one has reached out, asking for money. This is personal. Whoever took her wants something other than cash.

A week has passed with no news. I'm losing my mind, feeling her terror deep inside me. I'm so desperate that I've agreed to meet the one man I hate. Her father, the man I despise so much it hurts. I'm on edge, not trusting him, ready for a trap.

My father and his bodyguards are behind me, while I have a car of men in front of me, and Vinny and the driver in the middle with me.

"Did you read over the information on Jonny?" Vinny asks. Jonny was dirtier than I thought. He never stopped trying to advance himself, even if that meant ratting on the men higher than him. He had no honor. His ambition to rule would have been his downfall in the end, if he hadn't decided to go after Aly.

I nod, making an effort not to allow my leg to tap up and down. "I did. It will come in handy."

I'm back to watching out the window, searching for snipers who may want to take us out. The meeting is too easy. My father believes the reality of Mancini losing his daughter has him ready to cooperate. I don't trust him to be that man. My father is placing his personal values onto him. But if neither of us took her, who would unite the two strongest families, instead of pitting us against each other?

T ENSION IS HIGH AS the Mancini and Rossi dons and I meet. Everyone else is left to sit outside, since this is a family meeting. The smug smile is hard to keep off my face when not even Coy and his father can attend. Those feelings are momentarily fleeting until the door is closed.

"First, you steal my daughter, and then you lose her!" Mancini barks, baring his teeth. His hand slams down on the table, shaking it. His mouth is pinched, his hair wild like he hasn't combed it in days. No one flinches at his outburst.

My eyes narrow on him, trying to read his body language, searching for a flaw. He plays it expertly well. My heart almost believes him. When comparing our features, we're not that different.

"Would Coy take her as retaliation?" I ask, biding my time until I break his heart with the news of his son. Then we will see how good of an actor he is.

"Not without my permission. He's loyal," he says with disdain, as if implying that I'm not loyal.

"Was your son loyal?"

Mancini is much older than I've kept in my memory. Even though I've seen him through the years, each time I think about him, I get the same image of the day we met.

"You are nothing more than a street thug who thought he could marry a mafia princess," he sneers at me. "I want one of your daughters for my son." He looks straight toward my father, pretending I don't exist.

My father may welcome one of Mancini's daughters and treat her as one of his, but Pierre Mancini would never return the kindness.

"Never," my father says, his voice firm. They would have to pry one of my sisters out of his dead hands for him to turn one over to our enemy.

"Then why would you think you could take my only daughter?" he questions. "You have four. Pretty ones too."

I want to squeeze Mancini's throat in my hands, but I refrain.

"For a man whose daughter is missing, you don't seem to care that much. You're more worried about gaining a daughter to replace her," I say.

"I thought we wanted to bury the hatchet, so to speak," he baits us. "Wasn't a truce initiated at the same time you stole from me?"

"You're getting old, and everyone is stealing from you. Even your own son." I watch for his reaction, getting ready to pounce with the news I can't wait to give. I've built this moment up, ready to poke holes in everything he has said or done.

A low growl erupts from his chest. I want to keep hitting him until I break him. One piece of information at a time.

"I want your blessing for my marriage to Aly, in return for information that will save your life and family."

"You come to my meeting, insulting me by asking if one of my men has my daughter. Implying I would be hiding her. And then you ask for my blessing? Show me my daughter alive, and then maybe I will consider it."

"Don't be a fool, Mancini. We are trying to make amends for the better of all our families. It's a fair trade. Your daughter already loves my son." My father speaks trying to place reason in the room.

"I will not be a puppet to whatever you are planning. When I find my daughter, I will come for Luca." I watch Mancini stand up, ending our meeting. The folder in front of me sits untouched, no one even eyeing it. What's inside are pages and pictures of his son selling him out to allow Jonny to take his father's spot. Jonny gave the FBI all the information they need to put his father away. Leaving him the lone shark in the water. He was no longer happy being a capo, but wanted the title of boss.

"We will find your wife," my father reiterates, his hand on my shoulder.

Stepping out of our private room, our men surround us. This is not a truce, and the war has escalated.

Moving toward our cars, a package with a red bow sits on my car's hood. I stop as my men inspect it. It could be a bomb.

"It has your name on it," they confirm.

"Open it." Inside the box is a small memory stick. Picking it up, I roll it in my hands before shoving it in my pants pocket.

ONCE I'M HOME BY myself, I place the stick in my computer. I wait to see my wife's beaten face or limp body, but instead, it's a video of me.

It shows me lining up my slingshot, the rock sailing through the air. It has our whole altercation that changed my life. I try to think what the significance of this video might mean to someone other than me. It was the day my life changed for the better. I turn the video off, unable to watch my two friends get shot in cold blood.

Picking up my phone, I call Vinny. "Find out what happened to my old foster parents," I order.

CHAPTER 32

LUCA

ANOTHER TWO DAYS GO by. I have more blood on my hands as I try to follow every lead. My old foster parents are dead. Died of old age. I've even begun looking up some of the other foster kids I met throughout the years. Through it all, there is no evidence of my wife anywhere.

My phone rings. "What?" I answer, annoyed that I'm being interrupted while I think of different avenues to explore.

"Luca?" Aly's sad, terrified voice rings through my ear. Her trembles claw at my soul, marking her as mine more than ever.

"Aly, are you all right?"

My heart nearly bottoms out when she doesn't answer.

Seconds tick by before a deep, altered voice responds, "I'll text you an address. Be there in thirty minutes, no weapons, no hiding behind anyone else. Otherwise, she won't live to see your first anniversary."

I grit my teeth, swallowing my retort. My blood swooshes through my veins as I prepare myself to fight. Getting into my car, I wave off my men. Spinning my tires, I leave home, heading toward the address. I rip through the streets, breaking every law until I'm parking in front of an old, abandoned house. My old foster house, to be precise.

The neighborhood has fallen apart more since I left. Most houses on this street are boarded up, appearing vacant. Knowing it was my past that placed Aly in danger crushes me. I promised to protect her no matter what, and she fell through my grasp. She doesn't deserve to pay for my sins.

I walk in, and I'm slapped across the face with memories. The house has aged but is the same. The living room couches hold a few additional holes but haven't moved. The pictures on the wall still have the same photographs as they did sixteen years ago.

On the coffee table, there are pictures of me and Aly together. They start when she was sixteen and continue to our wedding. I was a fool to believe that no one knew about my infatuation with her. A sick feeling that I have been played begins to take root in me. My whole body and mind are in turmoil, fighting over how I fucked everything up. I should have stayed watching Aly from the sidelines. I should have never given in to my craving. But then her face appears in my mind, and I know saying those things would never make them true. If I were to do it all again, I could never hold out from seeing her and taking her. She consumes me to the point I have a hard time focusing.

"Show yourself," I holler out. How dare they make me come alone, then hide from me. They wanted me here. Now it's time to do business.

I almost swallow my tongue when I watch Coy walk out, clapping his hands.

I fucking knew it.

"Just couldn't handle her happy, could you?" Not only did I watch Aly through the years, but I was forced to witness Coy pick up the pieces when I couldn't be there. The times he drove her home because I couldn't risk being seen. The time he held her in his arms, carrying her away to safety, when I was the one covering their backs. I hated each time she would look at him, and I wondered if she thought of me.

He laughs freely. "I was stupid to think I was alone in wanting her attention. I have to say you caught me off guard, and no one else has ever been able to say that."

"Well, you have me here. What now?"

"This isn't my show. I wanted a second of your time before the real fun begins." He smiles at me, laughing like I'm the joke. I don't even know what he means, but I let him keep talking, hoping he'll drop some clues. "What information did you want to trade with Mancini?"

"What do you have in return for me? You're obviously a middleman and have no bearing on whether Aly is safe."

"You see, Aly was promised to me when I turned twenty-one and became a made man. But I can see you love her, and out of my respect for her, I won't kill you. If she dies, her blood is on your hands, not mine. She's not here because of me. As soon as she said 'I do' to you, I stopped having a say."

"How about a truce, man to man?" I counter. Who knows what the FBI has on everyone? Maybe it will come in handy one day.

He holds out his hand, and I take it with a firm shake. "Jonny was backstabbing everyone and giving information to the FBI so he would be the one left standing at the end of it all. Rumor is they're coming for you tonight."

Coy nods, his face serious. "Thank you."

I watch him walk out of the house and am left with the thought, What the fuck?

"You clean up nice," an unknown voice says, appearing in the hallway.

"Not as nice as us though," another voice comes from behind me.

Turning around, I think I'm seeing ghosts. My two friends, Scott and Jay, from when I was ten years old are now standing a few feet from me. I swear it's them. Their voices have changed and their looks have matured enough for me to question myself.

"You're dead." It almost sounds as if I'm in awe. I watched them take a bullet, both of them. I saw their lifeless bodies.

"Mancini saved us, took us in. He gave us shelter, clothes, a job. We owe him everything, while you ran away to be someone's puppet. We never forgot about our friend who left us high and dry. Mancini didn't even have to pay us when he gave us this job. We welcomed it, waiting for our revenge on you," Jay says.

I'm at a loss for words. I thought my friends were dead. I had their deaths sitting on my shoulders my whole life. Guilt ate at me further each day as I thought about when they were alive. The realization that I was right and Mancini is behind Aly's disappearance, hits me hard.

Mancini has been waiting in the reeds for a moment to strike. Instantly, I see his plan laid out in front of me. This is the diversion. Aly is my trap. Whatever he's doing right now, he didn't want me there for backup. He knows my once so-called friends will kill Aly, and I will be blamed, while he becomes a victor in whatever plan he's set out right now. The families will be forced to side with him when there is no opposition.

I hear a scream and start to follow it, when a Glock is shoved in my face.

"Don't move." Scott holds the gun to my temple as Jay drags Aly out in front of me.

She's dirty, dried blood on her face and clothes. Her hair is disheveled, her eyes wild.

My "friend" Jay brings out his phone. I can hear my sister swearing at Mancini. "You lost Aly the moment you chose your family. I'm giving you a do-over. Aly or your sister!" Mancini yells as I watch him on the screen, holding onto my sister's hair while tears stream down her face. The live video zooms out. They're in the middle of our driveway, dead bodies lining the area. Aria tries to get out of Mancini's grasp, but he pushes her to the ground.

"Take me," I say as my breath whooshes out of me. I can't breathe as my eyes go from my wife to my sister. It feels like déjà vu from our reception all over again.

"Dying is the easy part, Luca. It's living with the consequences that's hard," Scott sneers, moving the gun that was pointed at me to Aly. I could overpower them both, but that won't save my sister.

"How do I know you won't kill Aria?" I ask, trying to give myself time to think of a plan.

"Mancini wanted to take her himself. I heard his younger son, Romeo, is thrilled about breaking her in," I'm told by Jay.

"Luca!" my sister screams.

"I'll give you three seconds. Three..." Mancini counts with a leering grin that I can see from this far away.

In that second, I logically grasp the notion that I can't save my sister. Even if I choose her, there is no guarantee they won't kill her as soon as I leave this house. The thought is sickening, and I already feel like Nicoli Rossi wasted his time on me. I should be choosing my sister no matter what, yet I know I will pick Aly. I can guarantee her survival over Aria's.

"Two..."

I already hate myself before I say the words out loud. My father deserves to kill me. I won't even fight him on it.

"Aly," I say, defeated, at the same time he ends his countdown.

"One."

My sister screams before the phone turns black and gunshots spiral into the room where we're standing. Aly is flung to me, and I push her to the ground. A bullet speeds past her and grazes my ear before another one hits me in the shoulder. Both bullets were for Aly and would have hit her if I didn't move her. Falling to the ground, I cover her with my body while I respond with gunfire. I have no problem dying for her.

Bullets spray the room, hitting walls, pictures, furniture. I'm hidden by a small portion of a couch. More gunfire sprays the open space of the living room. I can't place where the extra bullets are coming from, and neither can Scott nor Jay. They begin to fire randomly in the room, giving me time to focus my aim for each shot. The front door flies open, and Vinny steps in, looking terrifying as hell. He walks in, unafraid of the bullets flying throughout the room. He goes straight toward the guns firing back at him. With one bullet each, he ends their lives without any remorse.

"You okay, boss?"

CHAPTER 33

LUCA

ALY WIGGLES FROM UNDER me, reminding me that my whole body is splayed over her, trying to protect her like a human shield. The shocked expression stays in her gray eyes as she stares back into mine.

"Luca," she rasps, her hand going to my face. "I thought I would never see you again."

Seeing her brings up a whirl of emotions—hate, love, relief, happiness, and anger. I give her a low grunt in response. I want to kiss her... and hate her.

"We need to get out of here," Vinny says, cutting through any chance of us having a moment. Picking her up, I toss her over my shoulder. I can maneuver her better this way while I keep watching for anyone else who might pop up. She wiggles in my hold but never once asks to be let down. I puff my chest out, liking this agreeable side of her.

Stepping outside, I see one of my bodyguards is standing on alert between Vinny's and my cars. I move Aly from my shoulder to cradling her as I place her in the back of the car on my lap.

"Compound, now!" I shout. "They're going to kill Aria."

Vinny stomps the gas, and we race toward my home. As each second ticks by, I start to feel helpless. We're too far away to save her. I try calling my father, but he doesn't answer. Each and every person I try, there is no getting through. I start to prepare myself for the worst. They could all be dead. From the phone screen earlier, I counted ten bodies.

My leg taps in a steady rhythm. I'm not used to having to wait for anything. I glance over Vinny's shoulder to make sure he's driving as fast as he can. I should have taken the wheel, but then Aly would have been by herself back here. Nothing I have done will fix everything that needs to be. I can feel a headache starting to push its way behind my eyes. I hold Aly in my lap, never expecting I would be able to do this again. My head stays straight toward the front window, even when I hear her start to talk.

"Luca, I'm so sor—"

I cut her off, "Not right now." I refuse to let her in. If I see her face, I'll cave. I already can't stop holding her.

She recoils like I've slapped her and tries to move, but I keep her in place. I need to hold her to prove to myself that this is real. To give me one last memory of what we could have been.

I don't want to go back to our wedding reception night feelings, not ready to hear she no longer or never has loved me. With my sister on the edge of being killed, I can't deal with that too. It would break me. Never in my life have I thought I could be broken. But I never knew love as I do now. I never knew the true meaning of family until it could all be taken away. Coming to the compound, I see red and blue lights fill the area.

I curse under my breath.

"What should we do?" Vinny asks.

"Drive in." I won't be scared away from my home.

Lowering our speed to a crawling pace, we pass a bunch of parked cop cars. I watch as Mancini is placed into a cruiser, his arm bandaged, but no serious wounds.

The car stops, and I move Aly to the side, all while ignoring her. I can feel her eyes on me, making it harder than I thought. Without a word, I step out of the car. Vinny follows my lead, leaving Aly to herself.

I quickly scan the area, searching for my sister, afraid to find her as one of the bodies already covered with blankets.

"Luca Rossi."

I turn to see a cop. He's not one who's on our payroll. I don't recognize him. He doesn't give off the vibe of being a dirty cop either. He smells clean and ambitious. One of those types.

Eyeing him up and down, I observe he's my height and built like a brick shithouse. This guy spends way too much time at the gym.

"What?" I pin him with my glare, daring him to give me trouble.

"Your sister is this way. She's been asking for you."

I almost step back in shock. I was waiting for him to arrest me or show me a warrant.

I allow him to lead me past a group of people, happy to hear she's alive but still worried of the condition she could be in. I see my mother, then Aria. Aria is sitting under a blanket, her hands clenching the material to keep it around her tiny frame. My sister sees the two of us walking up, and her face brightens. I've never been so happy to see that smile. I don't deserve her kindness.

Standing, she runs toward me, her blanket still draped around her. "Luca! How's Aly?" My sister is a saint. I chose my wife, and she's worried about Aly without any grudges toward me or her.

Meeting her in the middle of our large driveway, I respond, "I am so sorry, Aria. I've let you down. I don't deserve your faith in me." My sisters mean the world to me, and more so to my father. If I were a lesser man, I would fall to her feet. Instead, I stay stiff, wishing I could show her how much she means to me.

"Don't be silly. You made the right decision. I could never live with you choosing me over Aly. I never want anyone's blood on me."

She glances past me, and I turn, following what has caught her attention. She smiles shyly at a cop. I want to take her arm and move her away but remember he was probably the one who saved her.

She steps toward the cop. I watch as they stand with an awkward tension rolling between them. There's something off with their body language.

Fuck, I'm losing it. Shaking my head, I officially decide I need sleep. I'm starting to sound like a woman and making something out of nothing. Running my hand down my face, I come up beside my sister.

"How were you saved?" I probe, glancing between her and the cop before staying on his uniform. I take note of his last name—Fox.

My sister startles at my loud voice and takes a step away, unaware that I'm picturing the cop's head on one of my targets.

"They followed Mancini here and came just in time." Her voice is too dreamy, and I want to stomp all over it.

"If they followed him, why didn't they stop this before it got out of hand?"

"Is there a bigger question you would like to ask me?" he dares to ask me, stepping in front of Aria, but the Italian in her refuses to be sidestepped. My sister narrows her eyes on me, but this is for her own good. If our father was beside us, this fucker wouldn't have a job tomorrow.

I'm about to unleash hell, when I hear Aly calling my name.

CHAPTER 34

ALY

LUCA LEAVES ME IN the car as he runs to find his sister. I immediately miss his presence. The darkness engulfs me, masking that I exist. I've been a fool, thinking my father loved me. I've always been a pawn to him. I never realized it until I learned he was the one who took me for his revenge on Luca. I now understand fully why my mother tried to distance us the best she could from him.

Tears fall down my face as I realize I messed up the best thing that ever happened to me. Luca. I was an idiot to let him walk away. Using my palm, I wipe the silent tears off my cheeks. Cautiously, I step out of the car, taking in the compound grounds. It's like a movie set for some bloody horror movie. I search for Luca in the dimly lit area, blue and red lights helping to cut the darkness. Each step I take away from the car, I walk into casted shadows and colored lights. I could slip away into the night, but then I would be leaving a life that I want.

Between the sea of people, Luca is nowhere to be seen. Searching in front of me, my eyes collide with my father through the back window of a cop car. I freeze midstep. He glares, not happy to see me. His mouth is turned down, disgusted by my mere presence. The way his cutthroat stare is watching me has goose bumps traveling down my spine. Then he smiles, sitting up straighter and pretending to be morally honorable, like an arrogant asshole.

Turning from him, I increase my pace, but I can't help the impulse to look back at him every other second. His mouth opens in a laugh with his head leaning back before he puckers his lips, sending me a kiss.

The red and blue lights don't brighten the night as I thought they might. I could describe the area as calm chaos. No one is moving too fast anymore, but everyone has a job they're doing. I'm the lone soul wandering around trying to find Luca, the man I hope I can still call mine.

I won't take him saving me or holding me as a sign. Luca is loyal to a fault, and it could all have been out of habit or out of the need to kill me himself. Or worse, torture me for the rest of my life. I've seen what an unhappy marriage can be like in this lifestyle. Once you're in, the only way you're leaving is in the ground.

"Luca," I call into the darkness.

"Aly, over here!" Luca waves for me. He's standing beside a cop and his sister. He doesn't take one step toward me, staying still, and I have to walk the full distance to him. I swallow down my nerves, ready to accept my fate. Instead of hatred in his eyes, there is something soft and warm. Slowly, his sister steps away, giving us some space, while the cop goes on with his business elsewhere. Luca wraps me in a tight hug, catching me off guard. I try not to allow my hopes to rise too high. Mafia men do not forgive; it breaks my heart that I have placed us in a situation like this. I wanted to explain on the dance floor, but the words refused to leave me.

I breathe him in, that scent of gun powder and wood lulling my heart with little effort. "I'm sorry for everything, Luca. I don't know why I accepted the poison from my father. You have to believe me that I would never use it to hurt you or anyone in your family," I sob. The whole time I was gone, it was the only thing I could think about. It is the one thing I regretted the most. "You have to believe me that I love you." He could ask me for anything, and I would do it to wipe our slate clean. I cry harder, clinging to him.

The seconds slip into minutes as I hold on to his stiff body. As time passes, our chests begin to match each other with their rise and fall. He stays silent, making me sick and dizzy with worry.

On a sigh, he says, "I should have never doubted you. And for that, I am sorry. I should have believed in us, and none of this would have happened." Raising my eyes to meet his, I see Luca is staring at me with the same pained expression as I have. His hand glosses down my hair. "But it doesn't erase the past."

I sob harder into his chest. His arms hold me, allowing me to cry. I want to feel safe and secure, but his body stiffens further as he continues to talk.

"You have placed me in a difficult spot, Aly." He swallows, staring into the dark night. "Our fate will have to be chosen by the family."

"Do you still love me?" I'm willing to walk to my death if it means he will fight for us.

"Our fate has nothing to do with love." His arms loosen around me, his body moving away from mine. "What I can promise is I'll come for you no matter the outcome. You are my wife, my responsibility."

My body trembles. I know enough, that if his family wants me dead, Luca will be the one that will have to do it. I'm his responsibility no matter what. I try to stay strong, not wanting this to be harder on him than it already is. Or at least, I hope that I'm right in that assumption.

"Please fight for me," I whisper taking his cold hand into mine. I place a kiss on his knuckles, then flip his wrist over placing a kiss on his wrist like he has done to me before.

"You need to go with my mother and sisters now," he says, gruffly.

A drop of wetness falls on my cheek, then another on my forehead. Lifting my face to the night sky, it begins to rain, washing the blood from the ground. Luca's mother smiles softly at me, and I pray this could be an omen that there will be no more blood on anyone's hands for tonight.

B Y THE TIME THE police leave, my eyes hurt and I'm exhausted, but the adrenaline running through my body makes it impossible to sleep. Luca's father immediately called a meeting, and now everyone is waiting for it to start. Men began to walk through the doors, an unusual sight, because normally they keep to the outside. It's unnerving, not knowing how retaliation will begin.

I try to gauge how Luca's mother responds to know how worried I should be. She gives away nothing and ushers her daughters and me into the kitchen, warming milk for all of us. We stay quiet, words never leaving us. I feel incredibly guilty for everything that has happened. If I had lady balls and stood up to my father at our reception, maybe I could have altered the last couple of hours and days. I'm grateful for the silence and the cup in my hands. I'm able to stay in my head, and the urge to fiddle is gone with the warm milk I hold.

It takes hours before Luca returns. His clothes are dirty and wrinkled, and his arm has been bandaged up. I hadn't realized he was hurt. His eyes are crinkled around the edges, with a slight redness to them, but he is still handsome as ever.

He gives me no sign as to the verdict. He glances toward me only for a brief moment before he's going to his mother and giving her a kiss on the cheek. After, everyone leaves us alone.

My hands shake around my now cold mug.

"Come on. Let's go get you cleaned up and have the doctor check you out." He begins to shuffle me away. I can't help but wonder if he's wanting to clean me up before he's forced to kill me.

"Can you still love me?" my voice hitches. Not knowing is killing me inside. Dread clings to every part of me.

"I could never stop loving you, Aly. That is my biggest problem. It's why the family had to meet. You blind me, and I could never make the judgment call that would be needed."

My heart pounds ferociously, still not knowing the outcome.

Luca gets down on one knee. "Aly, will you be my wife?" he proposes to me for the first time. Relief floods my heart.

"I have only ever loved you, Luca." Falling to my knees, I kiss him. It's full of passion, deep with longing. I pull him closer by threading my fingers through his hair. In amongst the chaos of the night, our hearts find their way back to each other. I try not to second guess our reunion, wanting to believe in us with all that I have. Can it be this easy?

Ending our kiss, Luca holds my shoulders, helping me up.

Leading us to his bedroom, he delivers the news of my father's death. With no one nearby, he had a heart attack that caused his untimely death. I don't believe it was a heart attack. Someone put a hit on him. I feel like I should be sad, when instead I feel relief and anger. It seems too easy of an out for him. But I breathe easier, knowing he won't be trying to finish what he started.

The next day, I'm the one who identifies my father's body. His wife is too distraught over the fact that he left her alone in this world without him. His sons, my half-brothers, are unable to identify his body, because they're not eighteen yet. I can't help but wonder what will happen to the Mancinis now.

CHAPTER 35

ALY

L UCA HAS BEEN WORKING all hours of the day and night, leaving me by myself even to sleep. I try to understand, but I crave his closeness at all times. The dark used to be my sanctuary, but now I hate to be alone in its blackness. I've been having nightmares, waking up in cold sweats but not remembering the dream. My heart races like it did while I was held captive. Just like all the times before, I jolt up from the depths of sleep. My pulse is accelerating at an alarming rate. My hand goes to take comfort in Luca, but his side of the bed is cold and bare.

Luca doesn't sleep much, but I was hoping he would be in the room. Peering over toward the chair, I hope to find him sitting there, watching me sleep. Being alone does nothing to calm the pounding in my chest. I flip the covers over, needing to turn on the light to scare my demons away. As I swing my legs off the bed, the door opens slowly in an attempt to be silent. It's the tiniest motion, like someone is trying to sneak into the room. My breath stills. I should scream, but what if they think this room is empty?

Pound, pound, pound.

I don't dare move a muscle, trying to remember if there is any weapon close for me to use. Staring through the darkness, blue striking eyes collide with mine. They hold my attention, neither one of us moving. Sluggishly, Luca walks fully into the room. His face is shadowed by the hoodie he wears, similar to the night I first saw him. This time, instead of his fingers rising, his gun comes up. My breath vanishes from within me, wishing this was a bad joke. Time will never be able to erase the treachery of my doing.

Carefully, the gun keeps moving past me and is placed on the dresser. I'm forced to suck in a breath, realizing that my guilt is still eating at my soul. My ears begin to ring with the sudden adrenaline rushing through me. The red light on the clock reads 3:00 a.m.

My wide eyes trail Luca's movements as they adjust to the dark. His features begin to come in clearer. I can make out dried blood on his face, and his lip is twice the size it normally is.

My hands come up to my mouth. "What happened?" I ask, but then it dawns on me. I saw Jonny in a similar state one night long ago.

"Have you been made?"

He doesn't say anything, but he takes off his hoodie and shirt. There is deep purple bruising on his torso. I may follow Luca anywhere, but this life still frightens me.

"You're imprisoning us to this life forever."

He pauses, his thumbs wiping over his swollen lip. "You are lying to yourself if you thought otherwise before. Does it scare you?" He's intently staring at me, similar to when he first started to come around me.

It takes a few seconds for me to answer. "Only if it scares you." My heart is still beating rapidly and refuses to slow down.

He pushes down his pants, standing before me fully naked. Leaning over me, he kneels on the bed. Naturally, my body is pushed toward him with the mattress dipping. I sink lower, his arms coming down by my head. Luca has caged me in, hovering over my petite frame.

"Why are you scared of me, wife?" he asks gruffly.

"You forgave me too easily."

His fingers brush down my face. "That's not true. Look at how you're punishing yourself."

He picks up my hand and places it over the left side of his chest. The familiar thud that helps lull me to sleep keeps a steady rhythm. His mouth opens, then closes before he sighs.

"I feel you deep in here. It hurts when you hurt. If you stop living, I stop living. That is how it works between us."

I can feel my body ease into the bed, my pulse starting to find its natural pace. "Promise?"

Moving my hand up, he kisses the top of my knuckles. Delicately, he turns my hand over to kiss the inside of my wrist.

"I love you, Aly Rossi. Enough to kill for you, but I would never hurt you."

He leans down, placing a hungry kiss on my lips. Deep down, I rationally know this. I don't know why I've been so worked up over it. It's like I can't get a handle on my emotions. Everything is heightened. I try to make my kiss light, not wanting to hurt where he's bruised and swollen. Growling, his hand slips behind my neck, cradling it, and moves me harder to him. Our tongues mix in a fight to prove how much we love each other.

His lips move to the side of my mouth, his teeth dragging my bottom lip out. He nips at it before going toward my neck. His hand slips under my silk nightgown, moving tenderly up my sensitive skin. I want him to touch me everywhere. I want to show him how much he means to me. My chest rises and falls in short, rapid movements for an entirely different reason now.

"This is how I like my wife. Needy... and greedy," he says between kisses. My heart rises with each skim of his lips. Hope blossoms for our future. We're going to remember these days with admiration and warmth in years to come.

My hand goes down, grasping his already hard cock. He pushes himself into my hand deeper, and we both sigh out.

He cups my breast, his fingers pinching at my sensitive nipple. "You still want a punishment?"

I'm lost in thriving on Luca. My body needs him to feel in control.

"Yes," I pant, dropping his dick, because I can't concentrate on stroking him while he's touching me like this. His thick cock falls onto my thigh and brushes against my skin.

He lifts my chin. "After tonight, I'm yours, and you are mine. No more being scared of past ghosts."

He captures my lips again. We kiss with no giving up, with his hand cascading down my body, stopping at my panties.

"Take these off." Moving to his knees, he gives me space. I like him watching me. His shoulder muscles are strained, like he has to restrain himself from pouncing at me. It gives me power and courage. I'm held captive by the hunger in his eyes, spurring me to keep my little show up.

Playfully, I begin to move them down my legs, alternating each side I pull. My body twists as I slip them down a little lower. I can feel how wet I've already become. Luca always sees me, and right now is no different. When my panties get to my knees, he pulls them off me before spreading my knees apart.

He chuckles. "You're damn wet for a man you're frightened of. Could it be you like pretending you're scared of me? Do you like when I'm forced to sweep in and save the day for you?" His eyes gleam with arrogance.

He likes being in a higher position than me. He wants—no, needs—me to need him. How am I realizing this for the first time?

He pulls my body down, and I slip closer to the middle of the bed, my feet at the edge, ready to dangle off if I move another inch.

"Open your mouth," he commands. Straddling my face, he slides his cock into my mouth. I wrap my lips around him, my tongue twirling his shaft. I'm completely at his mercy. When he moves back, his cock slips out. "Kiss it."

Moving my head up, I place a kiss on the crown before he places it back into my mouth. He tastes salty from the pre-cum, and it has me sucking him harder, wanting him to lose control.

"This cock is yours, Aly," he grunts. "My heart is yours. My soul is yours. Do not ever forget that."

He slips out of my mouth and pulls me higher as if I weigh nothing at all. With no warning, he thrusts into my pussy and begins to fuck me. It's animalistic in the way our bodies slap together, our breathing heavy, and all that can be heard are moans and grunts.

The expression on his face will forever be held in my memory as the night Luca gave himself fully to me. There is no hiding behind a mask, his emotions on full display. This is the night we became confident in trusting each other.

ALY

I 'M SHOCKED HOW EASILY my life has merged with Luca's. We see his family often, his sisters becoming some of my most favorite people. Instead of always being alone, I have family and friends everywhere. The feeling of being loved and welcomed is a complete one-hundred-and-eighty-degree difference from how I grew up. In the beginning, I was afraid I wouldn't like people around me constantly. It's not the case at all. I look forward to seeing everyone.

Luca comes in from his day at the office, as he likes to call it. No blood on his hands or clothing—always a positive sign. I jump up, happy to see him, and place a peck on his lips.

"I have the results from the doctor," I say in greeting.

"I thought no news was good news?" he questions, concern lacing his posture.

"There was one small thing they found. A parasite of sorts," I continue, trying not to allow my smile to break through.

He comes to me, his hands grasping my shoulders with such tenderness. "What do we need to do?" He searches my eyes.

"I suppose we will have to love it when he or she is born."

His body tenses. We've never truly talked about having kids; it seemed like everyone else talked about it for us. It shouldn't come as a shock, considering we've never used any sort of protection.

"A baby?" He sounds dumbfounded, like this was never a thought in his mind. "Is that why you were so sick a few weeks ago?"

"Probably." I can't hold in my smile growing by the second as it stretches my face until it hurts.

"Holy shit, we're going to be parents." He lifts me in the air and twirls me.

"A little Luca Junior."

"It could be a girl," I remind him.

"Anything you have made, I will love. This is the best type of news. A new generation of Rossi." He lets my feet drop. "I have a surprise for you too," he tells me.

Lifting a brow, I wait for him to continue.

"I have moved your mother here to live with a full-time nurse."

"Really, when, how?" I ask flabbergasted. I've been trying to see her but the home was still not letting me in.

"I didn't want to get your hopes up, until it was a sure thing. And if it's okay with you, I want to try bee venom therapy on her to see if it helps. I've been researching it, and I think it could benefit her." He's talking a mile a minute, excited about his news.

I'm so happy I could cry. Bringing my arms around his shoulders, I hug him.

"I love you."

His hands run down my long hair. "I would light the world on fire for you. You're what makes me see the good in life." He kisses me on the head. "Go see your mother. She's downstairs waiting for you."

"Thank you." I give him another hug. My heart is so full, it hurts. Luca really has made all of my dreams come true.

Luca

I STEALTHILY FOLLOW MY sister, Aria, trying to convince myself I'm projecting my worries for my wife onto her. Except, I'm not worried about Aly. She's safely tucked away, and I have cameras on her at all times. After all, she is carrying my baby. She deserves protection.

My sister is acting sketchy as hell. She's wearing a baseball cap, its brim pulled down as far as it can go. Her body twitches, and she keeps checking over her shoulder.

Since the night Mancini tried to kill her, she's been off. My phone buzzes in my pocket. Slipping it out, I try to keep my eye on the phone and my sister.

Aly: This is not a drill. My water broke.

Cursing to hell, I slip my phone back into my pocket. My sister is gone from my view, and I can't wait around to put Vinny on her trail. I make a mental note to look into what she's hiding once my baby is born.

Stopping, I circle around. I'm the only one back here now. Shaking my head, I jog back to my car. All of my thoughts are on Aly, needing to be there for her.

Gunning the gas, I'm anxious to find out if we are having a boy or a girl. I still have a hard time believing I'm having a kid. I never thought I would find someone compatible with me. When thinking of the future, I expected to take over the Rossi family business but then give it back to the firstborn son of my sisters. Children were never a thought in my mind.

Aly makes me see a future past myself for the first time in my life. Even as a young boy, I honestly never expected to live past my youth. But here I am, ready for my next chapter. Prepared and ready to defend my family against anyone who tries to hurt them.

The End

Want to know if Luca and Aly have a boy or a girl? Download their bonus epilogue here: https://BookHip.com/BSVCPQB

* * *

Continue reading for the prologue of the next book Sinful Daughter

Prologue – Theo

"I've never claimed to be a saint, but you, il mio peccato (my sin), will destroy me," I rasp into her ear. She wiggles under me, making those beautiful moaning sounds only I get to hear. The room is lit enough I can almost make out the smile on her lips.

The party echoes around us, and I wish I could kiss her in public. I wish she wasn't planning on marrying someone who wasn't me. Twisting her hair around my hand, I yank it toward me while biting down on her neck. The desire to mark what's mine is strong, with the need for people to question who she was with. Even when I know it could get us both killed.

She moves her head as I increase my pressure but moans harder. That's my girl. Aria Rossi has corrupted me. There once was a time when I was an honest cop, and I'd look down upon people like me. I strived to ruin their careers, but now no one could hold me back if it meant keeping her safe.

She is more addicting than heroin. Without her, my life would crumble. Yet, being with her adds to the cracking glass under my feet. In the end, I'll fall no matter what. It's just a matter of if I can catch myself before the fall and how deep the shards cut, as I hold on.

Continue the Dark Mafia Sins Series with Sinful Daughter.
https://books2read.com/u/m0KawW

E MILY BOWIE IS A USA today bestselling author. She's from a small town in Western Canada. It has been her passion to make characters come to life through her writing since she was old enough to put her thoughts on paper. She loves her white wine cold, her heels red, and her books spicy.

Read More from Emily Bowie

https://www.authoremilybowie.com

Acknowledgments:

T HANK YOU TO MY beta readers: Sara, Jerilyn and Rea. This was my first time writing in the mafia genre, and these girls support meant everything.

My editor Kayla at hot tree editing. Thank you for believing in me and all of your support.

My proof reader: Karina.

Jersey girl design for my covers.

Dark Mafia Sins Series
(Romantic Suspense / Mafia)

Sinful Vow: (Luca & Aly) kidnapping, forced marriage

Sinful Daughter : (Aria & Theo) enemies to lovers, mafia princess/cop

Sinful Kisses: (Gia & Romeo) enemies to lovers,

Sinful Bodyguard: bodyguard romance, coming spring 2022

Sinful Queen: secret baby, coming summer 2022

Steele Family Series
(Small Town / Romantic Suspense)

Stolen Moments (book #1) (Shay & Luke) Brother's best friend romance

Moonlight Moments (Book #2) (Kellen & Sloan) Insta love (fling to forever)

Bittersweet Moments (book #3) (Brax & Raya) Secret baby

Whisky Moments (book #4) (Rhett & Camilla) Enemies to lovers, Rock star romance

All books are designed to be read as a standalone. Although, characters do have a reoccurring role in each book.

Box set of the Steele Family series:

Standalones:

(Small Town / Romantic Suspense)

Pretty, Twisted Lies (Kiptyn's book):
Kiptyn McGrath:
Kellie Dare was never meant to be mine. We existed in two different worlds. Mine was dark, dangerous, and unpredictable. Her's held prestige, wealth, and promise. I was never her white knight but allowed her to believe it until the day she forgot she was mine. I quickly became the villain who would stop at nothing to keep her.

Bennett Brothers Series
(Small Town/Romantic Suspense)

Recklessly mine (book #1) second chance love
Recklessly Forbidden (book #2) small town romance
Recklessly Devoted (book #3) enemies to lovers, next-door neighbors
Box set of the Bennett Brothers:

Oakport Beach Series
(Small Beach Town / Romantic Comedy)

Crashing Heart (Crash & Piper's story) Summer fling/ falling for your boss romance
Southern Hearts (Danger & Haven's story) Friends to Lovers romance
Wild Hearts (Frankie & Deacon's story) July 28, 2021, second chance love
*each of these books is a standalone and can be read in any order.

Printed in Great Britain
by Amazon

14120787R00103